MW01075124

THE LADY

WHO LIKED CLEAN

REST ROOMS

The Chronicle of
One of the Strangest Stories
Ever to be
Rumoured About Around
New York

J.P. DONLEAVY

With eight
original illustrations
by Elliott Banfield

ST. MARTIN'S GRIFFIN
New York

A THOMAS DUNNE BOOK.
An imprint of St. Martin's Press.

THE LADY WHO LIKED CLEAN REST ROOMS.
Text copyright © 1995 by J. P. Donleavy.
Illustrations & design copyright © 1995 by Thornwillow Press, Ltd.
All rights reserved. Printed in the United States of America.
No part of this book may be used or reproduced in any manner
whatsoever without written permission except in the case of
brief quotations embodied in critical articles or reviews.
For information, address St. Martin's Press,
175 Fifth Avenue, New York, N.Y. 10010.

Library of Congress Cataloging-in-Publication Data

Donleavy, J. P. (James Patrick)
The lady who liked clean rest rooms : the chronicle of one of the
strangest stories ever to be rumored about around New York / J. P.
Donleavy
p. cm.
"A Thomas Dunne book."
ISBN 0-312-18734-3
I. Title.
PS3507.O686L3 1997
823'.914—dc21 97-5852
CIP

FIRST PUBLISHED IN THE UNITED STATES OF AMERICA
IN A HANDMADE EDITION LIMITED TO 175 COPIES BY
THORNWILLOW PRESS, LTD.
DESIGNED BY LUKE IVES PONTIFELL

THIS EDITION REPRODUCES
THE TYPE DESIGN & ILLUSTRATIONS
OF THE LIMITED EDITION.

FIRST ST. MARTIN'S GRIFFIN EDITION: AUGUST 1998

10 9 8 7 6 5 4 3 2 1

To

MARIA THERESA

VON STOCKERT SAYLE

Who Wore Her White Gloves
In The Garden

THE LADY
WHO LIKED CLEAN
REST ROOMS

WITH EVERYONE REACTING to and following trends and fashions you never know what's going to happen next in and around New York and especially in suburban climes like Scarsdale. But what worried her more than anything was that she might sink down so deep into the doldrums that back up out of them she might never again get.

On the day she felt this most acutely it was her forty third birthday. She got a bottle of Polish vodka, chilled it ice cold, frosting the glass of a decanter and while listening to Fauré's Requiem, spent a couple of hours knocking it back with a sardine paste she made with garlic and cream cheese and spread on pumpernickel bread. But she got so drunk she found herself sitting at midnight with a loaded shotgun across her lap, after she thought she had heard funny noises outside around the house. Then watching a bunch of glad facing so called celebrities spout their bullshit on a T.V. talk show and remembering that once someone told her how, when having quaffed many a dram, they turned off T.V. sets in the remote highlands of Scotland, she clicked off the safety, aimed the Purdey at mid-screen and let off the no. 4 cartridges in both barrels. And she said to herself over and over again as the sparks and flames erupted from the smoke.

"Revenge is what I want. Nothing but pure unadulterated revenge. But my mother brought me up to be a lady."

Her analyst said everybody was blasting the shit out of their T. V. sets all over New York and described her new behavior of following trends as good news. For in the wake of her divorce from her strong silent husband, who wasn't so strong nor silent, but at least never beat her up, she had become a T. V. addict and virtual recluse. And as her bank balance declined, she let the grass grow long in summer and the leaves pile up in winter. But she kept herself in shape with an exercise bicycle and a lady's set of weights and ate mostly salad and fruit. She felt she owed her spiritual survival so far to a twice monthly visit to antique auctions and the art galleries downtown and to watching the local squirrels romping all over the place and their clever antics in preserving food for the winter.

There was also the strange incarcerated girl who maybe had something wrong in the brain and lived next door and who through the tree branches appeared in varying stages of undress waving at her at least a couple of times a day from her bedroom window and she waved encouragingly back. But the joy of that doubtful human contact with this otherwise attractive creature with a macabre sense of humour didn't last too long when one day the girl raised both her hands together and there were hand cuffs on her wrists. When she went finally to knock on this neighbor's door, whom she'd never met, the door it was hardly opened and then slammed shut with a voice growling.

"Mind your own god damn business."

The only thing she thought that was saving her from an overdose of sleeping tablets were her own unexpurgated cogitations going through her head, which she thought must surely be going through the minds of a hell of a lot of other people all over Scarsdale. Especially when she'd see some of them close up on the train station on the mornings of her gallery visiting days. When it seemed the game they were all playing was to appear important. But not to let people know what you were really thinking, that you were really a horse's ass. Her analyst said when you did let people know you really were a horse's ass, that was when you really were emotionally disturbed.

She was, as she told the analyst, Mayflowered and in fact half assed socially registered, since her mother who grew up on a southern plantation was, but whose marriage to a socially unacceptable father got her kicked out of the society books. But this remnant of superiority, wrest away before she was even born, she always felt had left her with a mind of her own and to also go and marry someone unacceptable. Which, in her presently deserted state, she was really regretting now with her two grown up and alienated children at college. And she was smitten when overhearing her son say to her daughter on their permanently last visit.

"Pop at least got some fun going on now in his life."

She shrunk away like a leper upon hearing this and cried herself despairingly to sleep. Her marriage had come to an end when her television executive husband, showing signs of getting bald and overweight, had invented a laugh-a-second game show and started to get ideas about a helicopter pad on the front lawn. However, he started landing somewhere else when he met a young associate producer who according to society column gossip was not only an ex college football cheer-leader from down Mississippi way but was also Phi Beta Kappa and who at twenty five years of age still sported firm tits, big bright teeth and an ass and legs to match.

After being away nearly two months of nights on a shoot as he called it, Steve merely waltzed in one evening and with too much to drink, had hit her between the eyes with the revelation that he had taken an apartment in the city on West Sixty Seventh Street and was in love and wanted a divorce. And she got down to brass tacks right away, making sure that along with her reasonableness she'd give him a bolo or two to the plexus.

"Steve, don't look all annoyed and hurt that you're hurting me. You want some fresh young flesh. It's normal. I'm not going to complain. Nor take you to the cleaners for everything you've got."

"Hey honey, gee whiz, you know anyway I ain't got that much."

"You've already got the children eating out of your hand. Just pay all the bills till the end of this month and give me one hundred and sixty five thousand dollars in cash, and the house with the rest of the mortgage paid off, and except for your personal stuff, all the furniture in it. Of course the Edward Hicks's and the objects d'art my grandmother gave me, and the silverware, were always mine. And you Steve can go have all the fresh flesh you want so long as you and she never show your faces at the country club while I remain a member and where I may want to go play bridge to live out my sag tit old age respectably. O but you can also have your tank full of piranha fish I've been feeding."

She took off her rings and threw them at him across the room. Steve sat like he had been electrocuted on the spot, and suddenly turned to look around at something that would remind him he was still alive, and he saw the silver framed pictures of the children on the piano flanking either side of their wedding photograph and Steve put his hands up to his face and broke sobbing into tears. Then as if seeking comfort he got up, crossed the carpet she was also going to keep, and as he bent over to kiss her, she let go with another bolo.

"Keep your dirty filthy hands off me."

She always thought that emotional high temperatures

led to foolish assertions, which now started to come out of Steve's, instead of her mouth. Making the accusation that her mother who never thought he was good enough for her and was trying to get her family reinstated in the Social Register. And that nobody from her side of the tracks liked hearing where he'd gone to college.

Of course to her who'd been at Bryn Mawr founded on that premise that intelligent women deserve an education as rigorous and stimulating as that offered to men, nothing could be so ridiculous. And who these days could give a flea's fart about that long list of practically anonymous social register names even though they were registered at the U.S. Patent Office. As a child she looked through her mother's old copy to find the tiny drawing of a yacht with smoke coming out the funnel which gave with the words "on board" these people's addresses. And it was that that made her realize that some people with more money than anybody else could have the world their own way. Which now for her would be forever in the future, impossible.

She toyed with the idea of going to live in a small town farther upstate New York or into Connecticut to a place with a volunteer fire department, a variety store and a couple of yokels at whose homespun naturalness she could marvel. But somehow for the time being, things being what they were and Steve having given her what she wanted, plus his sympathy, she thought matters at least couldn't get worse if she didn't stray too far away from the familiar.

In Scarsdale she still belonged to a more than slightly snooty country club where she could have a game of tennis or golf or dine with a friend or frequent with older acquaintances to play bridge. And all of which would help control her increasing eccentricities. Sitting alone in a big house as night fell produced moments teetering between choosing life and death and were rough rough indeed. Her only consoling thought being, so why worry about me, me, me while the whole world is poisoning itself with radiation levels rising and venereal plagues coming down the pike that make you shudder, shudder, shudder.

There were days, too, when she could cheer up and think that life overall hadn't treated her that badly. At least the house she had lived in for nine years being built of brick and stone, the termites hadn't eaten the place down. And now above all, from whence she could drive to the station, park and take a relaxed midmorning train heading downtown to visit the auction galleries and art museums. And all she had to do for her peace of mind was make sure she sat on the side which avoided going past the casket factory sign.

One guy who was selling real estate to whom she turned in sudden distress for an appraisal of her property had while walking through the butler's pantry already tried to put his hand to take feel of her rear end and with her best weight lifting arm, she whammed him one with her left across the chops. She thought her reaction was a sign of the menopause coming on but her lady doctor said she was in enviable prime female condition. And could procreate another family if she liked. And with a smile she said.

"I no like."

Poor as she now was and getting each day poorer, she viewed with a bemused cynicism the fact that Scarsdale was often referred to as one of the richest communities in the United States, and plus had more than a smattering of social registrites and she wondered would they never dare as the Irish did on St Patrick's Day, to all in their white tie and tails, top hats and ball gowns, march up Fifth Avenue in a parade.

But now in her long lonely attrition of feeling discarded she had at least learned ways of coping, especially giving herself an interest in art nouveau architecture and her current usual twice monthly whole day of contentment looking at her favourite paintings down in the city. And except for her distaste in not finding suitably clean rest rooms, these forays were saving her life, with culture providing the best self preservative and refuge.

She also started reading a few of the on the scene male novelists but felt they were merely a bunch of repressed homosexualists using their pricks as pens. And all they really had to offer were truly highly unimaginative dirty minds which she herself, practicing her masturbation every night going to sleep, thought up which were twice as dirty as a dirty old man's thoughts. And was imagined whispered in her ear by a chef who once in Paris, and much to Steve's chagrin, came out of his kitchen to say she was the most beautiful woman he had ever seen and if she got rid of her *homme nul* she was with, he would make her an omelette she would never forget.

There was no doubt that her involvement with the arts had immeasurably improved her contentment. And now that she was getting used to it, she minded less being alone when she was alone. And in fact now felt her isolation more when out in public with other people around. But with her walked the images she loved made by the great painters, their colours and forms colouring and framing her life.

She made an overall assessment of her assets. And estimated that, at least for the time being, she could comfortably coast along for a year or two or maybe three. What the hell, she could even add another few years to this with something entrepreneurial, she wasn't that dumb. Besides, women owned more than half the United States which was proof, if proof were needed, that they were smarter than men.

In keeping the furniture and the house with six bed-rooms, maid's room, four and a half baths, a conservatory and chauffeur's apartment over the garage, and even empty as the whole place was, she felt as a divorcee she retained at least some kind of status. She'd inherited from her grandmother early American folk art among which were two Edward Hicks of whom, Fernand Leger had said, was a more significant artist than Henri Rousseau.

In the evenings she provided herself with drawing room fires and listened to Boccherini and Haydn and to the Mormon Tabernacle Choir singing Stephen Foster's sad songs. She thought she at least would, with her one hundred and sixty-five thousand dollar settlement which Steve had to borrow from a bank and with her just burgeoning business ideas, be able to make enough to survive if not get rich and to afford going on living in the house, which admittedly she was finding, as her Steve used to say.

"This god damn setup I'm telling you cost a god damn whole lot of money to run."

And there was no doubt now, as the money seemed to disappear through her fingers, that what Steve said looked to seem how it was going to be. Especially when a brief boyfriend who with an oversized prick, cured her permanently of blind dating and gave her crabs, and also borrowed and disappeared with fifteen thousand dollars.

Then quickly following, a leak in the plumbing and some slates slipping cost more than fifteen thousand dollars more.

And suddenly without warning the unthinkable but unmistakable calculation dawned. With her last bank statement staring her in the face over her breakfast coffee she agonizingly realized that she literally could not afford to stay where she thought she could and had now to soon make a final decision that this big roof with its many slates and new guttering over her head, and the lawns and shrubbery beds around it, which, even with a low priced half-assed boy gardener, were so costly to keep clipped and manured, were up for sale.

That she had tried to keep up the pretension of being lady of the manor now made her feel sadly foolish as she had on the day when the T. V. repairman came with a new television set and he nearly dropped it as he saw the old one and she remained mum when he expostulated.

"Hey what the hell happened."

But optimism was the feature of the day when a new surveyor called and advised that nothing needed upgrading. Indeed, the house situated elevated on a slight hill on two and a half sylvan acres with its imported handmade Welsh slate roof and stone facings, plus mullioned windows, and cathedral ceilings, made it a most desirable residence. And it was so described by the realtor who said selling was no problem and he would add the words "eye catching and charmingly English."

To her the house really had two special features which no one else seemed to give a good god damn about, but she always did, and that was a genuine imported Adam chimney piece the previous owners had installed. And upon which she often lovingly feasted her eyes while day dreaming sitting in front of her evening blazing fires. There was also a laundry shoot adjoining the maid's room which shot down to the basement washroom and which her kids had put everything else into except laundry, including baby chicks they were once got for Easter, and then garter snakes they caught to scare the shit out of Mary the Irish maid.

As she sadly analysed it now, it was clearly a house easier for her to sell, than it was for her, dribbling away her remaining capital, to afford to support. Even though her once socially registered mother had always said that the grandness of one's house provided a certain degree of pedigree in the case of those having none. But with the prospect of the house going and perhaps soon to be gone, and her restorative routines in abeyance, loneliness again was the killer. Even attempts to lessen it seemed to lead only to more loneliness. She even banged cups and bowls with spoons and clapped her hands and kicked and slammed an occasional door to make noise. It was like a contaminating disease, except of course she could eat garlic to her heart's content.

And now one or two old girlfriends from Bryn Mawr with whom she'd laughed studied and cried in those gothic grey stone buildings and who could have been thought more than acquaintances were now cancelling at the last minute plans to come pay a visit. And she'd find out that instead they did something that was to her dumb and dangerous like taking their kids white river rafting down the Grand Canyon.

Haunting premonitions seemed to sound outside her bedroom window when an owl mournful hooted in the big old oak tree which survived in its grandeur since Indian days. But worse, much worse, were her foolish last ditch dream ideas to create some sort of European-style weekly salon to which young artists and writers might come. So terrible was her one attempt at this that she could not ever again bear to think of it even as an object lesson. But now she knew what it was like to be threatened to be raped. And what the hell her long abstinence may even have invited it. And once she shouted out.

"Holy shit it would be a god damn relief to be raped."

However all such local cultural plans, except her own, died without a whimper. As in the immediate vicinity of Scarsdale it seemed to be an intellectual desert and anyone who wasn't already a bond salesman downtown in some big brokerage house was practicing carrying a black briefcase to become one. And foaming at the mouth to get richer.

Even the kid to whom she thought she paid a fortune to cut the lawn and whom she had brought into the house to push around some furniture and to whom she mentioned the provenance of an odd piece of object d'art, thought she was talking about the name of a new sports car when she mentioned Chagall. And she should have been warned as the previous time she had him in the house to take the sewing machine down from the attic while she was out cleaning up the chauffeur's apartment over the garage, he drank all her vodka in the refrigerator and also by amusing mistake, took a powerful purgative concoction thinking it was a liquor.

"Gee, Mrs Jones, I got to use your bathroom somewhere."

She laughed herself sick over this, knowing small amounts of this laxative could blow your bowels out, bang bang, as she did the guts of the T. V. set with her shotgun. And she convulsed helpless as he turned blue and green and made for the downstairs powder room and once within made it sound in there like the Russian revolution was going on. Which following that day seemed to leave him semi-permanently indisposed.

But then in the crazy contrasts erupting in her life, she found that she enjoyed like hell sitting on the lawn mower and making like a great racing driver at full throttle shaving off the grass and taking a few wrong turns also knocking down the shrubberies. After a few vodkas she even tried it one midnight careening around with headlights on, all to the great amusement of the girl who was illuminating herself with a flashlight in her window, but not to the neighbours across the road who phoned the police to whom she explained in her best Bryn Mawr.

"I hope you'll forgive me for suggesting that I rarely make noise and simply on that premise hope that I may be forgiven that which I have just clearly made."

"You're forgiven, Ma'am. But just let's have a quiet night."

"And you gentlemen I hope will advise those creeps across the road to mind their own fucking business."

"At your service, Ma'am."

When she woke up dry mouthed in the morning staring at the ceiling she realized she might be going nuts and even her analyst was recently worried. Should she now regret not having divorced her husband and dearly made him recompense alimony at least for every year she worked for him as a wife. It did not pay to be a lady. And wake, if she slept, to ask the walls of her bedroom, how do I get through this day. And if I don't, who's going to come to my funeral.

Her analyst now insisting she try to keep alive her remaining remnants of a social life, suggesting, in what seemed a last effort, that she send out engraved AT

HOME invitations and get those remaining of her friends to a black tie dinner party to which he and his wife could also be invited. When she demurred on the grounds that her divorced husband had kept all the friends they had, and they were now part of his glamorous T.V. life, he said that she would find that folk flocked to be at such things. Well she would find out. She ordered the invitations from Cartier but did wonder if her analyst asking to be invited was abusing his professional orthodoxy and that he merely wanted to canvas for patients.

Ah, but she had now to come back to her sober senses or risk permanently going off the rails. However, perhaps still allowing for a little foible here and there. Which was human enough. And as far as her analyst went, everybody wanted to meet people. He'd never seen the house but yet must know of its every nook and cranny since she'd talked enough about it over the months. Without of course mentioning blasting the shit out of the T.V. set for the second time, or the boy gardener doing the same to the powder room.

And what the hell, she could at least dare to blow a thousand or two of her declining bucks, to give a black tie dinner before she took an overdose of sleeping pills and could then find out where her spirit might then go to dwell. But meanwhile she thought she could count on a handful at least of her inferiors who would be curious and snooty enough to come to see how miserably fucked up, screwed up and hard up she was after her divorce. And her old South Carolina grandmother had once said.

"My dear, anticipation makes you stop looking back in regret but meanwhile, don't believe all this equality rubbish, your snobberies are the most preciously valuable asset you will ever have in life, cherish them well. Avoid unbrave men and when you're away from your own trusted lavatory, only go to the cleanest of places to take a pee."

And indeed if anything was a trend in and around New York, it was for women to seek out the damn cleanest of clean rest rooms in which the polish and shine might blind you. Then totally unbelievably everybody to whom she'd sent her engraved invitation came just as her analyst said. And producing from the twelve guests a nice noisy convocation over the Louis Roederer champagne and smoked salmon and caviar canapés. With the hired Hungarian cook and someone to serve at table, and the boy gardener recovered from his loose bowels parking the cars, and while doing this only churning up half of the lawn.

But with the best of her grandmother's silverware polished to a gleam, and a hired butler for the pantry and taking coats inside the front door, it wasn't your worst dinner. Except that during opening drinks when she lit the fire something had blocked the chimney and smoked them out of the drawing room into the chilly conservatory. Until the boy gardener in his best bib and tucker, and mumbling fuck this shit under his breath, managed to get it unblocked but not without getting gobbits of soot over her and her cerulean blue chiffon gown.

"Gee, Mrs Jones, I'm really very sorry."

Invited, too, was her own lawyer who may have been attending out of a sense of duty and whose wife, a viperess, had just begun suing him for divorce, and he said to her wistfully that his spouse was not a thoroughbred lady like her of course, and as an attorney he expected to be both legally and illegally lashed and trashed. And she was amused that her analyst after exchanging just a few words with her lawyer seemed like a scalded cat to eagerly get as far away as possible, but then with a big toothy grin button-holed everybody else.

Then running out of Roederer and somehow despite the decently respectable New York State champagne, the evening only managed to avoid the awful deadness of a wake with people's conversation remaining platitudinously polite. Alluding to what schools they'd attended in preparation for colleges from which they graduated. Nor did it pick up much over the mint sauce and lamb chops and spinach even as beautifully as the latter was creamed. She felt they sensed her panic in the overly energetic attempt she made in the brave effort to hide her lonely and impoverished fate. At departure approaching each couple suggested they would be back in touch with her soon. She did however feel that the effort of the dinner had been worth it all to at least know that she could in fact still graciously entertain. And also to learn that absolutely not one of them, and especially the wives, was anyone she could rely on with her ass backed up as it was quaking to the wall as she protectively held each cheek in each hand.

There were only two disasters. And happening at the same time and when she was on her way back from the kitchen through the butler's pantry after seeing what the cook had set on fire, which was nearly everything as melted butter was blazing on the stove. And then an old time admirer, whom she partnered in the tennis at the country club and with whom she'd nearly once had an inebriated two hour stand in a motel, grabbed her and pushed her up against the pantry sink, kissing her.

"Gee Joy, you're still really something."

And she would have allowed him some encouragement only that his sour wife appeared at the swing door and caught them in the act, giving them both glaringly dirty looks and mumbling something indecipherably threatening. Then as this husband and wife took their prompt departure, she headed out the hall behind them to make feeble excuses that Charlie was just helping to put out the kitchen fire, but his wife only slammed the front door and shook a ceramic pot off its pedestal to break on the vestibule floor.

But the party did produce a cheerful few moments

when they all got around the Steinway grand with their liqueurs and a bottle of priceless brandy that was thrown in free by the wine merchant. She belted out the notes on the keys and they sang their favourite Broadway hit tunes and as the brandy made itself felt, old college songs. And her grandmother would have been pleased at the gleamingly dark green ivy league nature of the proceedings, except that she didn't approve of colleges above the Mason-Dixon Line.

But in retrospect and further reappraisal all seemed to turn into what she felt was a fairly dismal swan song. With everyone drinking respectably too little and remaining tight assed. And when they heard she was going to sell, they said with more than a hint of nervous laughter that they hoped it wouldn't be to undesirables. But then like puppets all in unison, ten minutes to midnight they got up, proceeded out to their vehicles and with the car doors slamming loudly went home. But not before they got a view across the lawn of the girl in handcuffs up in her window illuminating a degree of her nakedness with a flashlight.

Ah, but there were to be big ole surprises. And who would have believed it, as she searched everywhere all over the house, to unaccountably find that a Fabergé silver tea caddy marked with the imperial warrant, considered by Sotheby's as extremely fine, along with an even

finer gold mounted Meissen snuff box delicately adorned with boar and stag hunting scenes, and both bequeathed her by her South Carolina grandmother and which were not unreasonable to think were irreplaceable, had disappeared. She didn't think the nightly hired help or the boy gardener would have a clue as to the considerable if not astronomical value of these objects but she knew someone, who included most of her guests, did.

She thought that that was the whole point of an engraved invitation and black tie was that you eliminated guests who had a tendency to steal. Or was it white tie that her grandmother had said did that. If she cast around with suspicions she thought immediately of Charlie's angry wife. But if this unpleasant lady was even being vaguely asked did she see them, she was sure she'd be in a slander and libel suit which would take her to the cleaners.

Pray dear god, that what really happened is she forgot she hid the damn things before the party. But she hadn't, they were there. On top of the small games table. Discreetly in the corner. But conspicuous enough under the lamp light. Her uninsured tea caddy and snuff box. Heirlooms, wiped clean and the silver of one polished by her own delicate fingers. And they were the links with her grandmother and more than what people might think were just there to be seen. And demonstrated that even without a husband she still had things that anyone would be more than peacock-proud to own.

But even finding herself alluding to the descriptive word peacock annoyed her in its use slightly impugning the elegance of her southern heritage. However, she knew that the loss ultimately wasn't sentimental but financial and also made plain her vulnerability. But if they were gone, and they were, all she was left with were her bitter suspicions as to whom it might have been who had taken them. Then worse, she wasn't so damn sure. But she was even desperately tempted to become *infra dignitatem* by giving the names of all her dinner guests to the police, which would produce headlines in the Yonkers *Herald Statesman*.

SOCIAL REGISTRITES
LOOT PRECIOUS
HEIRLOOMS FROM
IMPOVERISHED DIVORCEE

But she was brought up to be a lady. Yet holy cow, she was fighting for her life all alone. And who knows, and what a laugh, a legal case could produce a real big crowd back in her life. In court house halls of course. Which is no laugh. What the hell, maybe with luck one of her organs would infarct and necrosis set in. Or as she did these nights, examining her breasts she'd feel a fatal lump somewhere. It wouldn't stop her from being invariably polite, but she could die a dramatically lingering death.

At least she knew where she wanted to be buried. In the woods of South Carolina. In an old country cemetery out in the quail shooting wilderness of her grandmother's plantation and next to her in their family plot where chiselled monuments recalling confederate heroes of the Civil War were stained with age. And where one had to tread with care in the long grass. As occasionally it had become a favourite place for snakes to sun and you could step on a cotton mouth moccasin and promptly join those of the departed already resting in peace.

Although she had always vaguely disliked her name Jocelyn, during the dinner everyone shortened it to calling her Joy. A word now she never wished to be reminded of with so much of it missing in her life. Not only was it the last straw that her objects d'art had gone missing but during her marriage she always regarded them as a financial ace in the hole with which she could suddenly decamp by calling a taxi and merely popping the priceless things in her handbag. Of course then bringing them to Sotheby's she'd have to go hold her breath in some respectable hotel until they were auctioned.

But holy ole golly damn if this is what your guests did to you, not only would one be unexpurgated in one's thoughts but in everything she would now do in her future, including the selection of friends. Which alas the latter hardly seemed presently an option as the only person left with whom she sensed any rapport was the girl wearing her handcuffs in the window.

And so after chewing it over for forty-eight hours she said to hell with this bunch of so called old friends and reported the theft to the police. There was no doubt that after that she was now *infra dignitatem* with her black tie dinner guests. Everybody anyway had got so much like each other you could go get a whole new set of acquaintances in five minutes and have to travel less than four miles down the railway tracks to Bronxville. But then at bridge in the country club upon telling her partners, it dawned on her there could have actually been a burglary and that the night she had got the shotgun and ended up blasting hell out of the T. V. someone might actually have been casing the joint and now returned, had just waited till the guests went into the dining room to dine.

Anyway to hell with them all. She had always regarded the name Scarsdale with some wry humour, separating and reversing the syllables in her mind, and referring to this indeterminate area as the Dale of Scars which she felt best described what the place had wrought upon some of its inhabitants. She was also finding out first hand that the roofer, the plumber or the electrician could all behave like lady killers first and Einsteins next, and then could after a couple of useless visits trying to date her, then try to financially wipe her out with a bill.

But there was no doubting one god damn good thing. Property prices, just as the realtor Mr Goodway said, had not only kept their value but increased. The house and grounds were anyway a pretty damn nice setup. Lawns bordering the shrubs surrounding the house and several towering trees producing summer shade. And except for its one foot-amputating big snapping turtle, a nice pond too small for canoes but big enough to swim in.

"Mrs Jones I've been a realtor for seventeen years and I regard number seventeen Winnapoopoo Road as being *sans peur et sans reproche* in the category of gracious executive dream homes."

"Well I hope you're right Mr Goodway, or else it will be a matter of *achever une bête blessée*."

And as the flattering photograph appeared in the realtor's brochure, the house was finally described under the heading "ravishingly English and steeped in old world charm." The further details were equally couched in terms she might not have ventured to use herself. But at least they were in English and that the setting was tranquil and provided with its own little body of water on its full two and three quarter acres of rolling Westchester.

The house was sold within seventy-two hours as two buyers converged bidding against one another and it was auctioned for ten percent more than the asking price. She wept. But hers had really been just some tiny interlude of life vanishing away in what always remained a very anonymous community. Where no one would ever historically hear or care about whether she'd been there or not. She learned that the more empty rooms you had to go into and get depressed the more depressed you got.

Yet she still felt young enough within herself to enjoy the occasional *frisson* that a wild sense of danger gave her. Affluent now she formulated plans to fly first class to Paris in the Spring and stay at the Lancaster Hotel and then following hours long and leisurely at the Louvre from there to venture across the Seine and beseat herself on Boulevard St Germain and have a *citron pressé*. She would let her reading glasses fall down on her nose as she read the Paris *Herald Tribune* and do so as if she was so engrossed in her pleasure that she had no time to notice the world.

Then to London to stay at Claridge's, that red brick carriage house down a quiet side street of Mayfair. She would be alone and free and not just extra baggage as she had been once on a whirlwind trip when her husband who'd gone traitor to his creative principles, was trying to pull off his first deal catering to the low brow consumer. Steve had said then that it cost a fortune but a big independent production deal required to stay at these hotels where the top prestigious Hollywood agents stayed and you would rub elbows with them in the elevator if they weren't down on the Mediterranean hanging out on yachts as long as football fields.

Somehow as much as she liked the hotels, she felt Steve's attitude betrayed his underprivileged background just as did his allowing cartons of milk to be put on the dining room table. And she felt more than a little awkward as he tried to throw his weight around a little and then had it promptly thrown back at him by a waiter's exaggeration of attention and courtesy. But affluent as she thought she had become following the sale of the house, it was as if no one wanted to know her anymore. Even though she bought herself a new Jaguar car in racing green and had begun to routinely play bridge with the older women at the country club.

It seemed that in now being merely an apartment dweller in a modest building not that far away from the New York Central train tracks, her status was abjectly diminished. To go out for an evening she even got desperate enough to hire the boy gardener as a chauffeur to take her to the cinema down in Bronxville and wait outside to open the car door for her when the show was over. It wasn't because she wanted to put on airs but because her loneliness demanded safety.

"Hey, Mrs Jones, can I take you for a beer to the Town Tavern."

If the protocol was ruined with the boy gardener suggesting he take her for a beer it was instantly restored when she cut him dead with a severe instruction to be driven home. And all the way there, there was nothing more in this world that she would have liked than to have had a beer at the Town Tavern. Even to chewing a salty pretzel and tasting her favourite pilsner as it coolly descended her throat.

It was shortly thereafter that she vacated her terribly anonymous apartment with its sunless living room and two bedrooms, and moved to somewhere slightly brighter and slightly more quaint, and that she would also find less lonely, and it wasn't. Hoping it would give her children incentive to visit. But they didn't. And who now seemed entirely ungrateful for the financial presents she'd bestowed on each. Instead sending her a formal thank you note. She felt the distance growing from both, especially Ida, her daughter who was at college farther away in West Virginia and who was being feted by beaus in half a dozen cities.

Her son, Hugh, with a year left to graduate from Yale and a member of Skull and Bones had even become slightly conspicuous in protesting against the admission of women, which she took as another slight directed against her. And he'd cited how women were wont to behave, particularly one young lady who had previously been releasing gossip of their secret rituals she'd learned from a disenchanted Skull and Bones boy friend and as Hugh publicly objected, it was making him appreciably more conspicuous.

As she was now getting more solitary than she had ever been in her life, she found herself more than a few times feeling incarcerated as was the girl in handcuffs in the window. Even itching one evening to call the boy gardener to take her to the Town Tavern in Bronxville for that beer he'd suggested. Her greatest pain came as her children's college weekends and vacations now silently went by even without phone calls as they went to stay with their father who was, thank you very much, described as having a ball with his new bimbo and announcing their engagement to be married. As a pair they were even mentioned as being "out on the town" in a most recent gossip column along with the brand new news that the bimbo before she hit the New York scene, was instead of being a Phi Beta Kappa southern belle, had worked in the dead letter department of a New Jersey post office.

But it had to be admitted that all her ex husband had now was his big salary, which might not be big enough having moved from his less expensive love nest on West Sixty-Seventh Street to a costly apartment on Park Avenue with a big rent to pay. Plus now with an aspiring actress in tow who was an obvious grasping gold digger slowly sinking her teeth into both Steve and her acting career. He'd also made it clear to the children that it was he who was paying through the nose for their expensive college educations, and although he'd refused giving them American Express cards as he did to his bimbo, he was however letting each have one hundred and forty five dollars a week pocket money to spend.

But holy cow, now she was, as well as rent, also paying enormous storage charges on the furniture from the house in Scarsdale. It could end up soon to have been cheaper to auction it or give it away. And she was also without her own big lawn upon which she had many a summertime evening, with citronella patted on her backside and when the mosquitoes weren't too thick, enjoyed the freedom of a fresh air pee and also doing as her grandmother said, not to waste nitrogen down a toilet bowl. And was once picked out in the flashlight beam the handcuffed girl was shining out her window.

Cutting down expense, her visits to her analyst were reduced to twice a month. Hoping now to stop herself descending into depressions in her smaller confines, she'd collected a library of self-help books and tried to do some of what they said. But she found, having forsaken martinis, that her most signal pleasure and ease was simply to take two glasses of a medium dry sherry with potato crisps and assorted nuts and with a long playing Elgar on her tape deck she imagined herself staring out across the terrace of an English country mansion where deer and cattle gently grazed and you didn't hear the express of the New York Central roaring by.

Alcohol remained significant in her life, but she never again wanted to be reminded of making a pitcher full of very dry dry martini and kept ready in the refrigerator, which she and Steve were in the habit of quaffing when he came home from work and which finally developed into using nearly a whole bottle of gin, and had her daughter accusing her.

"Let's face it, you and Daddyo for a long time on your cocktail before dinner kick, have slowly been becoming a real ole pair of swillbelly lushes. It's going to make pop impotent and if that doesn't matter to you then it's going to ruin your complexion and give you a big fat ass."

It was the word swillbelly and an Australian term of getting a skin full, said with more than a trace of know it all superiority that she found so wounding and humiliating. However, now forsaken by her family and her habitation reduced in circumstances, she was still keeping her moral and spiritual head above water, and even in her most lonely loneliness she thought things could be worse. And indeed they got that way only too soon, like a sledge hammer landing on her big toe. With another toe to follow. Firstly, when she complained of the children not visiting, Steve then let go his own bombshell bolo to her solar plexus.

"Jocelyn, I'll be frank. Everybody thinks you might be temporarily emotionally disturbed. And may need help."

"What on earth do you mean."

"Well while you were still in our house the police had to be called. Cutting the lawn at midnight. Shooting the T.V. with a shotgun. Yeah. I got a call from the T.V. repair man. Jocelyn, the simple fact of the matter is the kids love you and adore you but think you could be dangerous and could kill somebody by accident."

"All I was doing then and am still doing now for pity's sake is hoping to keep intruders at bay while I am sitting alone listening to Elgar."

"Well maybe that's the trouble too."

"Well that happens to be pleasure but I'm sure it must be clear even to you that no one, including burglars are impressed by violent death anymore."

As she digested her former husband's news and advice over a few days, next came the other sledge hammer blow. She discovered that her capital from the sale of the house, put in the eager hands of a hot shot investment adviser and former acquaintance of Steve's who said he would build for her a high yield centuries surviving cathedral of finance that even her children's children would be lazing off. But boy, did that romantically awe inspiring notion, in now exactly eight months, go belly up.

The dud investments included a chapter eleven declaration in both a computer firm and an oil exploration company, never mind the up front first come first to profit piece of the action in an absolute certainty of a Broadway laugh and dance show to which she was invited to see a rehearsal and to which on its opening, *The New York Times* said an immediate loud phooey in an easy to read headline

SILLY SAD AND SINKING

And all revealed just after midnight when she found herself standing in a large gloomy drawing room of a yellowing brick apartment edifice overlooking Central Park which had emptied in forty-five seconds after that review became news. So much for the enthralling and romantic excitement of the behind the scenes of the theatrical world. Into the void of which she'd dropped nearly two hundred thousand dollars.

But the very worst belly up situation happened in backing an investment advisory service where at least a couple of dozen telephone lines were in action in rented space in the Empire State Building to which subscribers were supposed to flock to get confidential ultra red hot smart tips on the market. This operation was overseen by a former opera singer and his model girlfriend to whom the investment adviser took a shine and had been convinced that with their café society contacts and their knowledge of large money movements they could infallibly predict trends and could sell the advice to the smaller midwest players for big market kills. And if the name wasn't so conspicuous the model and opera singer would have called themselves "Insiders Anonymous."

But there was more than just the opinion of phooey in this deal. Plus the players big and small for a start played alone. And then in the interests of setting up a mega bucks big situation plugged into the European bourses, the three of them went flying first class to Paris on an all expenses paid trip to stay at the Hotel Bristol to make contacts and get ideas and where also it would give the right impression to big deal merchants which in dining in Paris's most fabled restaurants did as well. And to attend assiduously upon the latter they'd brought a list as long as an arm and a leg to designate where each evening could be topped off with Chateau d'Yquem and *fraises des bois*.

When she advised her adviser Theodore that she was thinking of suing him for indecent negligence and sneaky fraud and that instead of building her a centuries surviving cathedral of finance, he had in a mere eight months put together a cardboard shack of venture investment full of bullshit which in a blizzard of expensive dinners, trips and long distance phone calls, had wiped out the major part of her capital, her adviser broke into tears and nearly sobbed in the lobby shade of a palm plant in the Plaza Hotel while she had china tea with lemon and cake, and he had double whiskies and for all of which she paid the bill. He said he had two kids at college who might now have to leave and take menial jobs.

"O, gee, Jocelyn I admit the whole scenario spiralled down into a loss trend caused by a continued lackluster sentiment, but still down the line I can see some sign of turnaround with an up-beat recovery potential and with right now the time to take advantage of the real low investment prices."

"I have no intention whatever of ever giving you another red cent of the pittance I've got left."

But it was her using the words indecent and sneaky that seemed to scare the shit out of Theodore. When she told the details to her lawyer, who as it happened, through her grandmother's influence, was one of New York's most prominent and who had a big office overlooking New York Harbour, a tear came into his right eye while the left eye remained dry. Although he was stooped behind his desk from a recent back injury playing tennis he kept struggling up from his swivel chair to take in a view of the harbour and a large liner leaving and spoke over his shoulder.

"You know, Jocelyn, the sad thing about all this is that your adviser is in fact as decent and as honest a guy as anyone can afford to be these days. The only trouble being that with the best of intentions, and a heart as big as his imagination, he just didn't know what the fuck, pardon my French, he was doing with someone else's money and there is no point in trying to send him up the Hudson to Sing Sing."

"That is not my intention."

"Well, Jocelyn, that's what might happen. Of course it could have been predicted that the computer business was over-crowded but the company he'd invested your money in was reputable enough. But the real big problem, Jocelyn, is the investment team of the opera singer and his model girlfriend. You see, they took Theodore for everything too and left him broke and his fairly nice house is in his wife's name which means there are no assets to recompense you if your negligence case succeeds."

The financial debacle had now forced her to give up her new apartment, auction all her furniture in storage and sell at a bargain price her four point two litre Jaguar in racing green. Her lawyer's advice not to sue cost her two thousand seven hundred and eighty-six dollars and eighty-seven cents. She moved at half the rent into a place less than half the size and in the rear of what was once a house owned by one of the richest men in the community putting her ironically occupying a chauffeur's apartment over a garage.

And now the real truth dawned, that none of her tried and true friends wanted to know her anymore. She was old hat, considerably poor and out of the action for good. From now on she swore she would apply a new theory to her life, instant instinct. And do exactly what she wanted. It was too late to postulate in her unexpurgated thoughts that you should never let anyone and especially your financial adviser bamboozle you. And then if he does, don't go to a lawyer about it because in the most confidentially nicest way he'll victimize you further. And O God there may be few laughs left in me but they're not never ever going to come out unless there is a laugh left in somebody else somewhere and he laughs first.

But there was even worse to think of. For the real prospect loomed, as to what might now become of her, shunned as she was and without a job. She could end up being a homeless person hanging around on a bench in the better air conditioned atriums of New York City. And plenty like her and just as dignified were already doing it. Her pair of Purdey guns had long ago gone to Sotheby's and only reached their reserved price and anyway, she could no longer afford to blow her T. V. set to kingdom come.

Her unexpurgated thoughts now had to be her favourite pastime except when she occasionally recalled moments of her young growing up days back in South Carolina an incident of which had been tragic too. At a high school prom she'd been invited to because she was one of the prettiest girls anywhere around and the boy who invited her, one of the most handsome, they'd gone expecting to be the beau and belle of the ball. And when no one all evening cut in on them in any of the dances to dance with her because she was such a knockout, she was crushed and the boy was desolate and she found him at the end of the night on the terrace his tears falling down into the magnolia blossoms. And she felt somehow it had all been her fault that she had not made flirting eyes or made herself seem glamorous enough and remained as she always tended to be, except for an odd occasion or two, faithful to her partner.

Now she'd be grateful if someone, anyone would only say some tiny flattering word, even as banal as I like your shoes they're cute. I would, I really would be pleased. But then after recalling such sad and sorrowful cerebrations she delighted in how ruthlessly vulgar her thoughts could get. She found herself thinking, you Scarsdale and Bronxville fuckers can go kiss my ass. Or better my socially superior twat. She felt, that in spite of her catastrophically reduced circumstances, she could still feel that in her taste in music and taste in art, she had something to be plenty superior about.

Out of her more than three quarters of a million dollars and after religiously imposing a budget accounting for every penny, she now had exactly thirteen thousand four hundred dollars and eighty-two cents left in the bank to support her for the rest of her life. Her only extravagance remaining, and modestly poor enough, were her trips down to New York to see the paintings in the museums.

But in her small isolated apartment and as the loneliness deepened around her life she briefly but seriously toyed with the idea of going lesbian and bought a book on the subject. At least it could be long term companionship without the horny unpredictability of a guy who could fall for a grasping conspiring bimbo.

But in becoming homosexual she couldn't figure out what role she might feel like playing. She sure as hell didn't want to end up doing all the washing, cooking and vacuuming, with the other girl wearing suits and a sombrero and heading off to her office with a briefcase. Nor did she want to be the bread winner up at six a.m., to be at the station at seven and then at a desk on Madison Avenue at eight. And especially after she saw what she looked like dressed up in front of the bedroom mirror in one of her discarded husband Steve's suits.

"O my god I look like I'd just stepped out of a faded picture from nineteen twenties pre-war Berlin."

But there was also the thought of the menopause down the road and getting fatter and fatter around the hips heading towards the age of forty-five. And she'd now seen a rented porno film of two big bull dykes bumping their naked skins together which filled her with considerable apprehension not to say a shudder of the flesh. Instead, while she had thirteen thousand dollars left she thought she would do community charity work, but after learning how high on the hog some of these charity cases were living, she realized it was she who needed the charity, or better, and fast as she could, a job.

But now came the bombshell. She may not even be able to find work. Her answer to such questions as what has been your salary history. My salary history has been zero. We're sorry. And they were. But at last she landed a temporary job as an assistant in a gift shop, in Yonkers. To her one of the strangest conurbations of all time. As you could never tell if you were in Yonkers or not. And when she asked.

"Excuse me, am I in Yonkers."

"Gee, Ma'am, I don't know what does the map say that you got there."

"It says Crestwood but I think I'm in Yonkers."

"Well, Ma'am, if you believe that sincerely keep it like that. All around here is Yonkers. But a lot of people wish it wasn't."

Although invariably sweet and polite, and good at gift wrapping, she got gently redundant when she and the owner both agreed that maybe some of the customers were intimidated by her elegance or maybe to see her there was embarrassing for too many customers from Scarsdale and some who knew her as a member of their country club, who gasped.

"Is that Jocelyn Jones from Winnapoopoo Road."

But the owner was pleasantly understanding and with a

large bonus under her belt she searched further and finally took up a stint of waitressing plenty of miles away from Scarsdale and Yonkers, getting there and back in an ancient third hand Volvo station wagon. And boy was this a quick way of waking up and starting to learn about life and about those serving and those being served. Rapidly finding she had no stomach for feeding the endless mouths, or watching those eat who were fat enough to go without a morsel for a month.

While trying to be good at her job, she felt so looked down upon, and that it was aging her rapidly. Her tits unmatching were already a little cross eyed but her left was now conspicuously sagging more than the right. Then finally on an overworked busy Friday night after she'd got several orders wrong and a complaining customer said she'd brought the wrong wine saying it was crap and it was a splendid vintage of Gevrey Chambertin, which she had herself already tasted, she held the bottle over his head and slowly poured out the contents as he sat stunned long enough for her to find herself announcing.

"I've been at Bryn Mawr you regrettable oaf and you're probably from the Bronx."

She of course didn't give a damn that she'd been at Bryn Mawr but her little exhibition of snobbery delighted her. However she knew this would be additional evidence of her emotional disturbance should Steve or her analyst whom she could now no longer afford, ever hear of it. And after being fired and the restaurant settling a suit for damages, she now more than ever began to think she should get way the hell out of this Yonkers no man's land area of Westchester and try her luck elsewhere. But elsewhere was upon any examination becoming a quick and lonely nowhere. Except perhaps New Hampshire where the people had a reputation for higher ethical principles. Her own background had only prepared her for telling at a glance the difference between the ormolu-mounted and floral marquetry of Louis the Fifteenth and Sixteenth. Perhaps the peasant European stock most of Americans descended from had got it right the first time and just made women beasts of burden and told their women to shut up, god damn it, shut up about facials and perfume and getting your hair done and get the fuck out toting that bale. Holy cow, dear dear granny, things are now getting rougher. They really are getting hard to bear. What do I do now. Having bankrolled my husband in the first place with your legacy and now being divorced without alimony. And she knew what Grandmother would say.

"My dear, need you ask. You stay and remain as you always were, a lady. But of course reserving being always ready to kick a bastard who deserves it in the balls."

Along with dreaming of escape she even dreamt of marrying again. She still got distant letters and not that long

ago, from the beau who was now a distinguished senator in Washington and who took her to his high school prom, wanting to know how she was and signed fondly with x's for kisses. But the truth was inescapable that the solution for women is to be not only filthy but disgustingly filthy rich sitting around in their boudoirs, bathing and nibbling on smoked salmon and chocolate from Paris. And to keep it a secret if they can from men. Who like to feel you need them. Because if you don't need them, either you or they run a mile.

She felt like a fallen woman who did nothing wrong. She had only let three other guys screw her during her whole marriage always restricting it to their being best friends of her husband. It was fast over in maybe twenty-eight minutes, the longest. She timed it on the watch Steve gave her for her twenty-ninth birthday. Now it was little consolation and comfort that even in her reduced circumstances other women, still married, were suspicious that their husbands might still want to jump her because, even with one slight sag in one tit she still retained with her daily sit ups her good figure backed up with her soberly attractive aquiline nose, blue eyes, high cheek bones and full lips.

When she dressed up to attend Sotheby's auctions in the city there was no end of attention she could still attract. And her best former girlfriends of which there were only two left from Bryn Mawr and whom she had only rarely seen, now felt like she might, being available, try to actually steal their husbands simply because the two times she was invited by both to dinner, vaunted vintages of wine were served.

"Gee John always brings out one of those chateau bottled this or that and decants it two hours ahead of time. He must really think you have a palate."

"I do."

And despite martinis, she did. Which Steve was fond of saying cost more to educate than going to college. Neither wife liked it either when she ate with gusto and was slim. And she really did have better than a good palate. She also knew and knew both these husbands knew and were thinking that along with her wearing chaste cashmere twin sets and a string of real pearls, that she could give them the best of blow jobs, to set bells ringing in their ears. Which practice had made perfect and which blow jobs, were regarded as a diplomatic way of remaining a virgin at Bryn Mawr. And what's more both husbands had already given her the eye, daring even to euphemistically mention a motel where they could meet for afternoon tea.

But holy cow even she thought she had got far too ladylike eccentric for impromptu roadhouse fucks, the hygiene of which could leave you feeling what the hell have I done. Especially as she had now taken up reading modern poetry and none of these stupid bastards had even heard of John Betjeman never mind Hughes or Heaney. Which had now become her indelible way of testing people's cultural quotient, finding out if, with all their vaunted degrees, they merely and really were only academic cultural numbskulls not ever having heard either of the architectural purist Adolf Loos.

But now too, and growing by leaps and bounds with her fortnightly visits to New York and the galleries, was not only her knowledge but her love of art. It had in these past worst of years given her a routine to anticipate and to live by. Even to making her lunch of tomato, cucumber and cream cheese sandwiches to stick in her handbag which she would eat with a thermos of weak china tea on a bench in the park, and feeding her crumbs to the sparrows and squirrels.

The lady at the membership desk of the Museum of Modern Art was so pleasantly encouragingly polite that even as impoverished as she was getting, she joined. And always enjoying to spend, especially on cold days, an hour at least in the lobby watching people go to and fro wearing their cultured expressions. The only slight disconcertance being that in the middle of looking at paintings she always found herself desperately needing to take a pee. And grandmother's voice in her ear.

"My dear, if you really have to, only clean, very clean rest rooms will do."

And as she discovered, the rest rooms of most of the galleries, always spotless, became in the case of an extended afternoon, to be simply overly used and not to her liking. All except for the great old mansion which housed the Frick, where there was something privately pleasant about the marble polished splendour of that building's ladies' powder room, albeit located in the basement but whose very lonely obscurity gave her unaccountable confidence.

But she had carefully picked out her available options of all those rest rooms which she made a habit of to attend. Outside the Metropolitan there was an excellently kept ladies in the nearby hotel. Which however as the doorman got to recognize her nearly scheduled visits, did look at her in a way she found, if not unfriendly, was certainly quizzical enough to make him think he couldn't remember her name and in return indeed made her pretend she was staying as a hotel patron. Although he and the other staff remained unfailingly courteous she did finally make a decision to seek other venues for taking her peaceful pee.

And presto, as she navigated elsewhere around town and other galleries, ideal places did turn up such as the Plaza and Pierre hotels, the latter being the less trafficked and most discreet. But the best of all were two up market funeral homes. Which, with a bit of a walk, she could frequent on both sides of Central Park. These she found were wonderful places, curiously chastening and comforting. Subdued in lighting. Softly and richly carpeted, boxes of facial tissue for tears and utterly shiny immaculate in their rest rooms.

And certainly life was becoming moderately tolerable on these days in spite of eking out her financial survival. Even if this was New York City, bourse of the world where even a smile has a price. And where so many of the dispirited wander. Where, too, so many of the unclaimed dead remain unknown, abandoned to Potters Field on Hart's Island off the Pelham Bay shore. But she still lived, seated on the shiny wicker seats, whooshing into the city on the New York Central Express and as she sat, thinking her unexpurgated thoughts through Crestwood and Fleetwood and Woodlawn and realizing there was a lot of wood this and wood that in the names.

She thought too that women didn't know what to do with themselves these days which could turn them into harridans. Hardly a female friend she knew wasn't miserable. Either mind dumb with children, or in the married condition married to an earnest toiler, or lonely unmarried in their successful career. And the misery of the feminist backlash over the whole god damn country was whipping everybody into bloody wretched minded submission either feminizing men or making them into bigger bastards than ever they were. And everybody desperate to diplomatically conform and afraid to call anything by its real name.

Even the faded memories of her and Steve's disaccord, seemed now not that bad at its worst. When she having moved the living room furniture around a bit which she knew would be to Steve's dislike, she'd stand there and say if the fucking son of a bitch comes home from his trip and moves that ashtray back exactly one inch to the left again as he did last week and all the weeks previous, I'll hit him over the god damn fucking head with a hatchet which with his psychopathic sexual obsessions, wouldn't be the only thing she'd be hitting him for. And she would hope Granny in heaven didn't hear her vulgar use of language.

But now having descended into the working class she wanted to keep reminding herself that she had seen better days that still could linger at least in her imagination. And it was only money that made the difference. That she'd once roamed her grandmother's great plantation by the sea and paddled her canoe amid the alligators and excitedly risked death from moccasins and hornet stings. But it was hard now to imagine that that same southern grandmother steeped her in her code of good breeding. And who always said if she said why can't I do that.

"Because my dear you were brought up to be a lady. A lady."

And she did, she remained a lady. But no longer to the full degree described in the dictionary. She now felt prematurely dumped as though she were being added to the geriatric scrap heap piling up coast to coast all over America. And maybe even in Canada where a lot of your folk, not having to worry about doctors putting their stethoscopes over their wallets and purses, are in better physical condition. And she was tending to become very British and would refer to matters disagreeable as a load of old codswallop.

She wished too that everyone in the country would wipe the phony smile off their faces. But to now attempt to change and struggle to again be a happy faced matron avoiding an *au blet* corpulence and gummy build up in life, simply was another humiliation she did not feel she could bear. Better to become reclusive and be shunned. Plus she found she was getting satisfaction out of avoiding people she used to know and felt it was at least an amount of satisfaction equal to the amount of guilt folk endured in avoiding her. But one thing she never expected to find was that money could end up meaning so devastatingly much in her life, and end up accounting for the mere fact of providing a roof over her head. Her now reduced circumstances had changed her life overnight from a brave busy existence of having been proud of who she was to now feeling apologetic. And then having sold her Jaguar and now her second hand Volvo, which corroded her independence further, reducing her to the demeaning condition of having to be seen standing in the rain to take a local bus. Her only consolation being as she got wet, that her grandmother had said.

"Ah my dear some of the very best people take buses. But perhaps in New York, only on Madison and Fifth Avenues."

However, a husband or two weren't shunning her and a wife or two were getting nervous. But at least her company could be better than having gone to investigate orgies going on in the back room of one of the notorious road house motels she'd heard of along the highway where briefcase carrying respectable members of the community were known to let more than their hair down. But a recent murder cured some of that notion. Plus the expectation of catching some filthy disgusting disease.

But could any multipopulated spree of debauchery be worse than moments when she got so low sinking in her loneliness that she merely sat as she did tonight, sipping an iced vodka and playing Mahler over and over again. Then at the last chord holding her hands clutched in her hair and sobbing at her plight. And so to put herself to bed. And good lord at twelve thirty a.m. reading and nodding off to sleep that sound she just woke to, was not Mahler but the noise of the door bell.

It had happened a few times before when she wouldn't answer. But her light was still on. And a couple of times when she did guardedly answer it at least produced an hour or two of companionship becoming a matter of suffering the embarrassment of silent panting desperateness of the only available guys who were always somebody elses husband, and always appearing too late at night when she was already abed under the covers trying to read for a while instead of masturbating herself to sleep. She could tell by the way the bell was ringing that whoever it was, was already tipsily losing their balance drunk at her door.

"Hey Joy, it's me Clifford."

And if she now stupidly answered it after being plaintively begged to do so, he'd nearly be unable to climb the stairs. But with her light on he was bound to yell again and her nearest neighbour, a refined elderly woman through the wall whose husband had recently died, might have a stroke. Then she knew, after having admitted him half heartedly welcomingly, that she would then find herself belligerently and uncontrollably accosting him and trying to send him home. Wondering, too, when he started trying to embrace and kiss her, if she might have to revert to under a small pillow where she now always kept hidden, one of her remaining prize possessions, a not so small 38 caliber Smith & Wesson Stainless

Steel M67 revolver sporting very upmarket marvellous looking gold plated bullets in the cylinder. A minute later as he stood on her living room rug after small inane pleasantries she let him have a gold plated piece of her mind.

"What are you after. Why are you here. At this time of night. What are you looking for."

"Hey gee sorry I didn't know I got you out of bed. It's a bit late, what is it one a.m. I'm just here I guess because I want to be here."

"Well that's swell for you suddenly deciding you've found a place to go after midnight. But for me that's not enough to provoke my hospitality. Why don't you go home to your wife."

"Hey gee, Joy, I don't want to sound trite this time of night but it's the god damn truth, she doesn't understand me."

"And you think I do. Well you're right I do. But you won't be flattered to hear about it, especially expressed in an unbiased opinion."

"Well gee, Joy, shoot."

"I'm going to. My understanding of you is that you're married to the most gruesome bitch this nasty world could ever have invented."

"What. Hey hold it. Holy Christ those are pretty strong words, Joy. She's the mother of two nice kids. Yeah holy gee. No kidding. OK, so maybe that's true. I'm too drunk to deny it anyway."

"But her bottomless trust fund helps keep you together in holy matrimony."

"Hey come on. That's way below the belt. OK, Celia's rich, but it ain't her fault she got trust funds. But I got a good job and salary. But I got to be away a lot with long hours. And I guess that's why maybe she doesn't understand me. Plus Celia just god damn outright doesn't like sex."

"And you want somebody else to supply the traditional standard home comforts of getting laid."

"Hey no."

"And if not that then getting a blow job. And that's why you're here."

"Hey wait a second Joy. Jesus Christ I'm here to come to see you. Not to get laid or blown. I really mean that."

"Well actually I really mean that I might consider it."

"What."

"Yeah really, don't faint. Giving you a fuck or blow job. If you put five hundred dollars on the table. And provided you don't take more than twenty minutes. Maybe we'll make that twenty five minutes. However, that is only when I see the five hundred dollars. And only then that I'll consider it."

"Hey holy cow. Hey come on Jocelyn, you'd do this. What are you doing. Hey what kind of girl have you become. Holy cow. Do you need help."

"More to the point, and holy cow, do you need or want

a fuck or a blow job. Because if you don't and don't have five hundred dollars I'm going to go back to bed. It's late."

"Gee you went to the best schools for Christ's sake. Bryn Mawr. Five hundred dollars."

"What has Bryn Mawr got to do with my price. Or is it too low."

"They didn't teach girls there that kind of arithmetic at Bryn Mawr."

"How do you know."

"Why would you do this Jocelyn. Right here in Scarsdale for christ's sake. Tell me why."

"Well to be geographically correct, it's not Scarsdale. It's Yonkers."

"Hey well at least you're right on or near the borderline."

"Well whether it's Scarsdale or Yonkers I'm offering you a fuck because I need the money. And you're not getting into me or anything from or out of me without it."

"Gee, hold it a second. I mean Jesus this is kind of a shock. Mind if I sit down. I got to re-evaluate this. Gee I'd be buying you pure and simple."

"That's right. Maybe not so pure, but damn simple. Five hundred for twenty minutes. Sorry I do believe I did say twenty-five minutes. So I'll give you fifteen seconds to think it over. But don't make yourself at home. Or maybe I better make that five seconds. Since I'm here in my pajamas. One. Two. Three. Four. Five."

"Gee Joy, you look good in your pajamas. You really do. Your figure still shows you're a real athlete."

"I said five seconds. Are you in the market."

"Yeah. OK, OK. Gee and I always thought you were a lady."

"Well that's what my ole mother, my grandmother and my governess taught me to be. And included with such tutelage was the tenet to be gracious to gentlemen, which perhaps is no longer the proper designation for men. However I can't see that in my directness I'm being in any way otherwise than gracious. Except that my present circumstances force me to make a gentleman pay for it."

"No. No. That's true. If you need the money. But gee five hundred bucks."

"Exactly."

"But well the truth is, Joy, I'm kinda short."

"Well gee, I'm sorry, Clifford. But the market truth is that in being a lady or pretending to be one, one does have a high price. Goodbye. I want to go to bed. I'm going down to the city first thing by an early train tomorrow."

"Gee, maybe can't you give me a shot of something. Just a jigger of that Jim Beam or vodka you've got there. And a little bit of ice. Then let me count out how much I got."

"If it's not five hundred dollars don't bother. And drinks are extra at five dollars. And just don't try to make yourself at home."

"Hey come on, Joy, you don't have a whore house

license to sell liquor. You know I'm not a pushy guy. Gee this is becoming the craziest night of my life. And I don't mind telling you this is all kind of a god damn shock. I mean you used to love the arts and outdoor sports. I mean you're a crack shot. Especially, you know, bang bang at quail when you and Steve and all of us went shooting that time down on big ole John's plantation in Georgia."

"That has nothing whatever to do with present business."

"OK, OK. But I knew things couldn't be good when you laid down your tennis racquet and your bridge hand and shotgun and quit the country club. But no kidding I didn't know you were this bad. OK, maybe recently no one's invited you or dated you to go out to dinner."

"Buster, no human body has even invited me to go for a god damn walk."

"But, Joy, holy cow maybe it's a fact that nobody knows where to turn in today's contemporary society. With the kind of things that are coming down the pike, I mean friends who already know each other got to stick together. A guy worries about disease."

"So does a woman."

"Yeah I know. That's why you got to find decent people to have intimacy with who you know and trust."

"Amen, Buster."

"Hey. Christ here I go searching in my pockets and

there goes a gold plated button off my blazer. OK. There. A hundred and thirty five bucks and eighty six cents. It's all I've got except for my American Express card. I mean I got a whole wad of charge cards. Look. And what's this calling me Buster."

"Isn't that what call girls call their tricks because they're all the same to her. And with only a hundred and thirty five bucks you're not a trick but still deserve to be called Buster. So you really ought to go home. And save your money."

"Boy o boy, this is really something. Please gee pour me another shot while it's still pouring rain outside. Gee for Christ's sake, no kidding Jocelyn. I don't know how to take all this. Is this some kind of backlash inverted attitude you got left over as a Bryn Mawr girl to the manner born in South Carolina."

"If I were to the manner born, it was just temporarily over the border in North Carolina. But I did attend a snooty girl's high school too and had a conversationally unexpurgated lesbian instructor who was sadly relieved of her post following telling her charges to make men pay for everything they get and whose dictum was, snobbery will get you wherever you want to go, so guard it wisely girls."

"Gee this ain't snobbery, Jocelyn, this is prostitution. You should find a guy and get out of this situation."

"I think maybe you should finish your drink."

"OK, but maybe you even should do yoga or go to a good dating agency."

"I did."

"You really did."

"Yes I did. And it so happened I met a real gem of a guy."

"That I suppose means he was god damn rich."

"Well he certainly had more than one hundred and thirty five dollars but more importantly he was kindly and thoughtful. However being a widower having lost his wife and four children in a plane crash, and that with my own estranged children our relationship got like a funeral. In fact it was. The two of us broke down in tears. But like tonight I'm getting well used to all kinds of existential situations turning up with guys."

"But Jesus, Joy, after a good marriage and coming from the kind of background I know you do, you're now turned into, and pardon the reference, into a woman of easy virtue."

"I think the reference you mean is hooker. And you're hard up for a screw. I mean I am most heartily afraid that your being hard up simply does not turn me on. And I'm simply doing you the courtesy of giving you a price and in turn providing a service."

"I am not hard up. And I never thought I'd ever hear such talk coming from lips such as yours. I could have had what I wanted, for no price, except a good time, from any of a dozen girls willing and ready at the bar I just left. And some of them damn good looking."

"Then go back there with your hundred and thirty five bucks. Because here you're short Buster three hundred and sixty-four dollars and fourteen cents. So you don't even get a smell of this little old gal. Not even from right where you're standing. And keep standing there."

"Jesus, Jocelyn, so long as we're calling a spade a spade, let me ask you again, do you need help or something. Don't you know with venereal disease the way it is these days, you got to be careful. But holy cow, that you'd do this for money. Wow, I shake my head, I really do, no kidding, you're not the same Jocelyn we all used to know when you were married to Steve."

"You're god damn right I'm not. And I'm heartily sick of every guy assuming that because I'm here living alone without any means of visible protection in this little walk up one flight apartment that I want them to screw me. And I'm just as concerned over disease as you are. But how do you know I'm not clapped up and with canine venereal granulomata and have got everything else in the books."

"Holy cow, Joy."

"Well I haven't and it's just a term I found in a medical book."

"Gee Joy I wish you'd cut the kidding."

"I'm not kidding. I'm forty-two years old and I just yesterday got fired working as a waitress. That's right. A waitress. Steve's wife and I who was at Bryn Mawr and lives in Scarsdale or at least on the edge. Not that I mind being a waitress. But as a waitress I was also getting unwelcome propositions. And I'm not getting alimony. And the menopause is coming."

"Hey ole honey you don't look like you're going to have any ole menopause. You just have got a little eccentric after divorce and maybe living too long alone. But you sure can do arithmetic. I mean holy cow what happened you maybe got a million for the house a couple of years ago and more at the auction of the furniture. You didn't lose all that money in dud investments did you."

"None of that is any of your damn business."

"OK. OK. But I could have as an old friend warned you against these guys building cathedrals of finance. Sure some stand up. But more than stand up go wrong wobbling on the foundations and end up a heap of rubble. Gee I sure do wish you were more friendly."

"That would be nice wouldn't it. But I don't see since I'm now living on the wrong side of the tracks, what there is left to be friendly about with anybody in this community where at my dinner party last year someone was unfriendly enough to borrow a valuable silver tea caddy. Plus an even more valuable Meissen snuff box."

"I don't believe it. No one we know would do a thing

like that. Not that I'm prejudiced but did you invite someone up from the Bronx or something. Gee you don't think you're kind of getting a few little ole bats in the ole belfry, honey. No kidding. This is talk like you're paranoid or something. But please go on talking. I like listening to you."

"Like hell it is paranoid. A new Ambassador to London not that long ago who invited the cream of London society when he took up his appointment, had every piece of object d'art in his drawing room swiped."

"Hey, no kidding. I thought the English were honest. Just shows you. The whole god damn world is tumbling down. Ethics, honesty, everything."

"And it's about time for you to go home."

"Gee Joy for ole times sake at least give me another shot and a couple of pretzels or something."

"Stop calling me Joy. My name's Jocelyn. And I don't have any pretzels. Go home. You're trespassing."

"Jesus trespassing. Holy cow. Boy this is a shock revelation in my life. You turning into a call girl."

"And you Buster who needs one, simply don't have enough money to pay for one so I haven't turned into one yet."

"My name's Clifford stop calling me Buster. Gee this is a god damn long stand up, and if you want me to be honest, a god damn honest conversation. I just don't happen to have a full five hundred dollars on me at the moment.

What's wrong with that. I mean are you still in the market selling."

"Yeah, I'm still in the market. And as I've already said, as soon as I see all of five hundred dollars I shall consider it."

"Then I'll owe you the rest. I mean I'll have it first thing tomorrow. I'll bring it right around here."

"Like hell you will. You're not coming around here again. And don't do that."

"Come on. Look at it. There it is. Waiting all this time. Hard as a rock. All full six and a half inches. Come on give the boy a treat. Hey what the fuck are you laughing at."

"You. Those are the most original words I've ever heard you say. Be a good boy. Put it back in your pants and go ask your wife to give the boy a treat. And I won't scream blue, pink and red murder for help through these paper thin walls and have my widow acquaintance and about twenty other nosy people wondering why I'm being molested and what your car is doing parked outside so that they call the police."

"Hey I got friends there, don't worry. Come on. Let's go. Into the bedroom. I'll bet you'll love it."

"Stay right where you are."

"Holy Jesus Christ almighty that's a god damn real gun you got there."

"You're damn right it is."

"Hey, Jocelyn, no kidding put it away. Guns can go off."

"You put your prick back in your pants and get out of

here because I verily assure you that it is going to go off unless you do. Move. Before I start screaming fire as well as rape. So I hope you've got friends in the fire department too."

"OK. OK. You win I'm faster than going. I'm gone. You sure ain't the old Jocelyn I used to know. Holy Jesus Christ all what I'm suggesting is only human."

"And all I'm being is humane in telling you to fast get the fuck out of here and suggest it to somebody else."

Clifford bent over his half zipped up fly as he made from the sitting room to the staircase landing tripping on the rug as he went. She did not know what on earth made her pull the trigger but it felt so appropriate to just ease her finger back on the curved piece of steel. His untidy retreat made her nearly laugh and the bullet passing his ear seemed to add speed to his departure. It also felt so damn good as the gun went off and the acrid smoke ascended up her nose.

When she turned on the hall light there was a hole right where the shadow of Clifford's head had passed as he went at breakneck speed to descend heavy handed on the banister, wrenching it loose and himself plunging from the third stair to tumble down head over heels eighteen more steps to the bottom. Clawing at the door in the dark to get it open and slamming it shut so hard it shook the whole building. Without a single sound of saying I'm going to sue you for spiritual maim and a faulty banister.

His car starting and roaring away with a squeal of tyres on the pebbles. A crash. O christ the drunk bastard has hit the nice maple tree hidden around the elbow of the drive. O lordy sakes is he dead. Or worse has he killed the tree. His friends from the fire department having to come cut him out of the crumpled wreck. O god thank the god I don't believe in. The car is starting again. And it's about time I made hot cocoa and retired to bed where my tiny room ever seems tinier every time entering it and reminding of the spaciousness of the house on Winnapoopoo Road.

Life had shrunk, keeled over and collapsed. Just like Clifford's penis. No longer shall I be able to feel freedom of space. From kingsize down to the now flea sized small single bed. The dressing table half against the window helping shut out the daylight. Good grief it squeezes the soul. And try to read. But now agonized over pulling the trigger. He could report to the police. Did I really mean to kill. Just as I did that bright sunny lonely day while I was out riding along a Carolina creek. My horse rearing. A grey black coiled cotton mouth moccasin, disturbed from sleep ready to strike my horse's leg. The relief one felt taking its head clean off with my twenty bore as the rest of its reptile body writhed on the rustling grass.

Why do guys always have to assume a girl is looking for a fuck when all she wants first is peace and quiet while she has a long hot bath and maybe day dreams through a fashion magazine. And a few roses would help. And an endearment whispered in the ear. And then maybe she wants a fuck. Another squeal of tyres. O god maybe he's back. No it's Mr Potter over the road. Who can't sleep and can't drive to save his ass. And doesn't mind ending up on somebody else's grass.

O happy days. Never have I ever enjoyed an ensuing silence so much. Or the distant sound of the last express roaring down the New York Central tracks into the city. Or maybe it's a freight train. But the unexpurgated depressing thought in one's head, that this is no longer a night for reading but for solitary masturbation. If only I can erotically concentrate. And avoid seeing Clifford's private part waving in my face. Which I guess in fact was every bit as big as he said it was and at least gives him a little credibility about something. Plus having played halfback on the first team at his boondock institution of higher learning out West. And O god there goes said a bit of my own snobbery.

Now after this debacle she would have to try to sustain the long continuous days of smoldering dissatisfaction. But it was quite unbelievable how much it could matter for the whole rest of your life as to where you went to college. And how even that impression could vary dramatically if you let people know you waited on tables to pay your tuition as she had had to for a couple of lean semesters ministering to her inferiors. And O god when you start examining the middle classes and upwards what a god damn smug and insultingly snobbish country America was underneath it all. And yet with jeans, coke and cigarettes we had culturally conquered half the earth and were busy as hell conquering what remained.

God damn hell the hot chocolate boiling over the stove. And is now going to taste burnt. And a whole night before sleep leaves tomorrow so far away. To go on living through the hours of deathly despair. Isolated in a growing and growing numbness. This is it. Go back to my bedroom. Already dressed for bed. Pull the shades down tight on the window. Face the hell of being unable to sleep. At least be able to see the colours and shapes of all the paintings one has now come to love and nearly know as one's own, keeps alive one last remaining pleasure.

Sanctuary. Sanctuary. Is what one needs and wants. Away from every plumber, electrician and carpenter who after his innuendos suggestive of carnal coupling were rebuffed, then was ready to take advantage of her lonely defenselessness to plot the rip off of the century to take her for whatever they thought they could get of her meager remaining funds. Maybe telephone that sad guy again. Before he marries his secretary whom he says has remained so loyal. He has an aristocratic air. His eyes alone told you he'd lost his wife and children. And he stared at you as if he felt you might bring them back.

All the happier times mouldering in my past. Gone as if

buried beneath the heaped anguish of loneliness. The very worst of all pain. Really I could become a hooker. Do it for money. What a damn good short term business it could be. By appointment only. Discretion guaranteed. Older distinguished men a speciality. At five hundred dollars a throw or blow it could become six hundred on Saturday nights and include a bottle of good champagne, background music, incense and candlelight.

"Stop. Shit. Stop."

Her shouting voice sounding so loud. Wake up that poor old lady more lonely than I. O god maybe I'd get nowhere as a hooker. My ass is still good, but my looks are going and maybe even gone. Even though guys on the building sites stopped whistling years ago I still get a whistle or two so must still have some attraction left. All that's needed is enough so guys can get it up. Treat each prick like being a frankfurter with or without mustard or sauerkraut. A preliminary massage makes them come sooner and there's a faster turnover.

"You've just had yours, Buster. Next."

And once during my first year at Bryn Mawr and on my first trip to New York, never having been on an elevator full of men going by express up to the fiftieth floor I blurted out that it was much faster going up than it was coming down. Flushing red as they all looked at me and two guys laughed as the tenth floor went by with forty left to go.

But the profession of whore had come at the wrong time along with lethal disease. And unless you really had to be a whore it did insult your children. Desecrate your college. Bring your sorority into disrepute. Make both your parents already pouring pills and gin down their throats, drop dead with shame. But gosh it sure as hell beat all for filling up the bank account. Please dear god, stop my unhelpful unexpurgated thinking as I try to go to sleep. I want to keep the present Cape Cod shingle roof over my head. Save this daughter of The American Revolution from being wrapped in polythene and all day sitting in the better atriums of Manhattan eating yogurt out of a plastic cup. Before life gets me in the tits like it does men in the prostate.

She'd nearly overslept on this sunny cool day of going downtown to the museums. And heard herself murmuring over this morning's breakfast. Onward Christian soldier even though you don't believe in God. And at least so far you're not constipated yet. Butter your toast. Drip on honey. Drink your juice. Sip your coffee. As each penny goes now. And is gone. What am I doing. What am I doing. Am I. Am I. Slowly gathering. Gathering sleeping pills. Sleeping pills. Towards night. To sleep, sleep, sleep. And forever rest in peace.

Who from Scarsdale would come to my funeral in Carolina and by my gravesite have to wear snake boots in the long grass. Take with me into the ground the terrible terrible truth. My bluff to Clifford might not have been a bluff had he had the extra three hundred and sixty-four dollars and fourteen cents. I might have actually let him breathe and prod all over me just to pay next months rent. Become a whore. Face the present reality of my life that I'm no longer the lady my mother and grandmother had so carefully destined me to be.

The first frosty chill of the year. Flurry of snow. Calling a taxi to the station. Locking her door with the memory of the memory of last night. The cemetery out in the woods. Twitching penises. Give the boy a treat. And O horror. There's Clifford on the station with a black eye and a conspicuous scratch down his face. And standing with his collar up in the cool Autumnal air. And just beyond the gentleman who like a British Guards Officer sports a military great coat and homburg hat and rolled umbrella. She'd seen him often before. The most conspicuous of all the passengers. And who was so clearly and endearingly American looking despite his disguise. Clearly Clifford's car clearly got busted up last night. Or maybe he was attacked by his wife. And as he saw her she shivered and he mercifully, along with two more husbands of her black tie dinner, hurried on down to the north end of the platform hidden by the other commuters from sight.

Out of a glowering grey sky white flakes descending blowing in whorls along the platform. The rails beginning to sing as the train came in, always seeming like a great throbbing monster roaring down the track. Climb aboard. A certain strange mix of people could change the atmosphere in the car. Could even be, some of them burglars with their overnight loot on their way back to the pawnshops on 125th Street or down Eighth Avenue beyond Hell's Kitchen. At least I have a copy of *The New York Times* with its reassuring small legend left top of the front page. All the news that's fit to print. To erase my own tabloid tidings with all my thoughts that are unfit to think. What would comprehending people do without this newspaper. To bring them in the morning some daily hope of better things. Delivered on their front steps or stuck in their door knobs. Moral arbiter. Champion of the oppressed and distressed. At least I fervently hope so.

Train stops. More of corporate America get on at Bronxville. Idle ideas. Out the window across the platform the First Westchester National Bank. Their inviting windows less than a stone's throw away. With my Smith and Wesson right now in my handbag could go in and menacingly request a stack of money. Hand over the swag. Dear me that doesn't sound right. I'll be a whore before I'm a bank robber. But this is the town where the old Gramatan Hotel once stood glacially like a castle redoubt atop its hill. It's said it was a favoured place for admirals, graduates of Annapolis to spend their retirement. They frequented a turret where they relived their commands at sea. Grandmother, her very few times in New York, instead of at the Waldorf, stayed there for the air. Taking tea on its verandas or a seat on the big sofa in its sprawling lobby.

Train pulls out. Rolls along the valley under the bridges where the Bronx River slowly flows. Sitting on the right side I miss the casket factory sign but see the haunting sepulchres of graves and mausoleums pass on the hillside of Woodlawn cemetery. Surprised at its sylvan beauty when one day I went to visit Herman Melville's grave. At least Clifford isn't going to tell his trust fund wife, hey holy gee, honey, I couldn't find a decent twat over there at that ole roadhouse so I went over to Jocelyn's to try to fuck her and took out my big ole tool to show her how it twitched and that ole bitch Joy, who'd shoot a poor ole armadillo dead, tried to sure shoot the shit out of me.

Maybe soon I really will go back down south. Where I remain in good standing a member of the United Daughters of the Confederacy. All such a waste of time north of the Mason-Dixon Line claiming to be anything anymore in life. Get away out of this uncivilized suburbia. So what if salamanders crawl up and down the curtains in the Carolinas and give Northerners the heebie jeebies, and bugs bite the shit out of one. But where men stand to respectful attention when a lady enters the room. And they really do try to click their heels. The Botanical Gardens. Another visit I must make. Maybe the Bronx isn't all that bad. Where this local train is now stopped at this station. Fordham University. Own a seismograph. Earthquakes only remind again that one is so painfully painfully lonely. Needing so desperately to talk to someone free of charge instead of being left rejected. Instead of at the rate of one hundred and fifty dollars an hour which one no longer could afford. Battle ships once sailed up the Bronx River. Now nothing but a small muddy looking flow of water meandering through lonely cold little meadows. All the historical things about New York one has yet to learn. Her grandmother said nobody who was anybody in her time lived on Fifth Avenue north of Fifty-Ninth Street. And not that it mattered as New York was socially forbidden territory anyway.

One always knows one is only ten or so minutes away from Grand Central when flashing past these grim ghetto windows. Washing drying on string strung across rooms. A gang of scattering kids running around a bonfire in a debris strewn street. The train descending into the blackness underground. The last fifty or so blocks through darkness. Dozens maybe hundreds of people living in the concrete rat infested interstices of these Stygian tunnels. The distant light bulbs dimly glowing across all the converging parallel tracks. Passengers stir, feel for their wallets, briefcases and handbags. She'd hurry out of the train. Avoid all the Scarsdale husbands. Take the Madison Avenue bus uptown. See all the women seated, youth in their face lifts, old age in their hands.

But today she'd splurge. Buy lunch at the counter in a drug store on Madison near 86th Street. A lettuce, egg and tomato sandwich, a piece of apple pie a la mode and a cup of coffee. Not cheap but nourishingly reasonable at the price. And the nice man the other side of the counter would say a pleasant there you go. O god if one could only concentrate, concentrate on just the very simplest of things there could be no end to the pleasures of life.

Climbing these familiar steps which she always felt went halfway to heaven. The Met holding an exhibition of her favourite old American painters with several Edward Hicks. The afternoon flies. Her feet tiring until three o'clock. She thought for a fleeting moment that she saw the sad grey haired but handsome man who'd lost his family. And found herself running. And then he disappeared around a corridor. She'd so many times thought about him since. His quite pleasant voice so full of sadness. On their first date out for lunch at the Russian Tea Room on Fifty-Seventh, when she insisted they go dutch over their modest meal he smiled and said no he'd pay, that the gods of manna had been good to him and nothing would give him greater pleasure than to be allowed to compensate them back.

There had been another suitor on the horizon briefly met through the introduction service. Nice as he was as well, he was just too preppy, shuffling forward in his loafers, his neck slightly craned forward as if walking like a duck. And she wondered what it was that looking so ridiculous and still young at forty-eight years old, how he could ever make any money. And yet looking so innocently stupid he made a lot. Drove a Lamborghini, and even professed love to her. And to finally get up her skirt even proposed marriage. All would have been fine. Except she discovered when his wife rang that he was already married with three children, two at college and a fourth on the way.

Dare she now go to her new favourite place to pee. But she must. She needed now to go and pee. And then following have late late lunch. Strolling past this a station wagon pulling up to one side of this pink stone building. Serious minded faces of two men manoeuvring a black long bag onto a trolley to wheel up a path from the sidewalk into a side door. A body in death on its last journey. Collected out of a hospital or from anywhere where people are allowed to drop dead.

As she continued around the corner to enter the front of this gracious and dignified sanctum, she hardly had enough money left for her own funeral. Through the lobby. Scent of burning incense. Never a shortage of names. Three reposing departed dead in their various suites. The ladies rest room just down the long hallway on the right. An ashtray and box of paper tissues on a polished table under the lamp. At least you know if you were brought dead to this place and your heirs could afford it, you'd be well looked after. But her own plans were increasingly serious to be buried back in South Carolina in the graveyard she so often visited there way out in the woods of her Grandmother's estate. And be together with great grand uncles who died for the Confederacy and whose tombstones had carved upon them the Confederate flag and swords hanging in their scabbards.

O god someone has come out of that back room and is coming heading directly at me up the hall. And when the sun comes shining even on this cool day, in my light green tweed suit. I'm not exactly dressed for a funeral. He'll solicitously enquire of me I suppose if I need any help. Or comfort in my sorrow. For whom do you mourn ma'am. I mourn for me. And Stephen Foster our wonderful composer. Who celebrated our country. And died right in this city penniless and in obscurity.

But this gentleman in his dark grey suit, white shirt and silk black tie, must see so many dead he won't remember seeing me alive in here before. Which he has. And I stupidly careless haven't got a name yet to say of a deceased. That I should have read first off on the notice board. One sounding Russian. Was it ending with a isky or something. O no. That's the name of a Washington strategic genius who tells us what's going to happen to the world and is always proved right. The kind of advice I could use now.

God, undertakers are so naturally so god damn nice. But better I avoid this one. Ah. Deliverance. At least I can go in this door for the moment. Clearly left open for somebody. And get out of his way. As I'm nearly sure he's seen me come in to have a pee before and might not be so god damn nice seeing me do so again and again. In here everything is certainly resting in peace. And not emotionally overcrowded. My god what beautiful choral music. Sounds liturgical and Russian. And O my god a casket. Someone is in it. I'll have to get out if mourners come in. The deceased, a man. Light flashing on the glass of his pince-nez. Undertaker is peeking in. Better to look like I'm doing something. Sign the visitors book. Invent a name and an address. O god someone could ask. How are you related to the demised whom the Lord calleth home. I don't even know the poor bastard. Accuse me of necrophilia. Or maybe just mild necromancy. Leering over bodies. Seeking news from the dead. How is it on the other side of the divide. Peek out in the hall. He's still there fixing flowers. As a left hander, scribble in the condolence book with my right hand. Then I can say that's not me. Laura sounds good. Laura Claridge Lancaster after my two favourite hotels sounds even better. Ponfield Road, Bronxville at least gives a modestly good address and make it a number in the early forties in honour of my age. The early bird catches the first worm. The first name to be written. But then I'm impersonating someone.

They could ask for my driver's licence. A lady never impersonates.

The man's still outside in the hall. I know he must know me from past visits to pee and is merely waiting for me to come out to tell me this is not a public urinal. Sit and take a load off my legs. At least I can keep vigil as no one else is over this dead man. Rouge disguising his ghostly pallor. Old worldy with a silk shirt, and diamond pin stuck in his black cravat. Has an intellectual face, a big nose. A twirled waxed moustache. O god what utterly serene beautiful music. A green glow of light behind the coffin. His condolence card says composed by Bortniansky, *Cherubic Song Number Seven*, sung by the Russian Republican Academic Choir. Voices sound as if they are waves in a great emotional sea. A low threnody in the trough. Rising triumphant at the crest. Clutching at the heart. A shiver going through one's being. A great ghost has come. Picks me up to fly out to the last and lost outer regions of space. But at this moment in this empty room one thing is for sure. Recognized or not. I've now desperately got to go and pee. And you in that coffin look just as lonely for friends as I am. You poor son of a bitch. But not as poor as I am. Which is such now that if I don't become a whore I'll have to become a nun. Seek solitude, simplicity, frugality and life without haste. But at least now that I know your taste in music it deserves my real name and address. Which I'll write beneath my phony one with my left hand. And I'll go kneel now and say an atheistic prayer.

Ah, at last, down the hall the coast is clear. And Mrs Jocelyn Jones in her light green tweed suit and purple scarf can stand up in the semi-darkness, and brushing down her skirt and braving the brighter light of the hall can. No I can't. O god the man in the dark suit is still standing there. O god. He bows with just a trace of a sympathetic smile. Now that's good southern behavior. Which being a funeral director may require be dispensed to interlopers. Maybe that's my solution. Go to mortician school. There must be female embalmers and undertakers. And if there aren't, some feminist group is soon going to sue that there should be. Braving the sadness everyday. Sweeping around in long black gowns and black rubber gloves. And working hard. But perhaps too much like a domestic slave. Which who knows what that could lead to. When first married, Steve said watching me do household chores like cleaning or washing a floor, especially if it required scrubbing and bending over, that it made him horny. And he was right, he used to try to stick it up me from behind with the biggest hard ons I'd ever felt, which made me turn around to look and it was at least an inch longer than normal and he finally had me wearing leopard skin lingerie trimmed with black lace to wash the dishes. Until one day, his eyes closed in anticipated ecstasy reaching for me with his jumbo hard on he pushed through the cellar door near where I was standing and fell headlong down the stairs.

As one tip toes across and down this hall a stocking is laddering. No one yet could have sat on this toilet seat today. One's thoughts have got so bizarre as one enjoys the marvelous relief to pee. Do they remove the piss as well as the blood out of the dead. Peer long and leisurely in the mirror at my deteriorating complexion. Powder the blemishes away on my cheeks and nose. And even now I get horny doing housework, and the more menial the hornier. Leave the ladies rest room before I start scrubbing this floor. And thinking that Steve is going to come barging in. So much for his emigrant peasant background where his female ancestors were beasts of burden and were still probably digging potatoes up with shovels and must have got so horny they were fucking each other on the dirt mounds left behind. Yet another smile from the dark suited man. Pass the door of the still empty reposing suite. The Russian voices still sounding the strains of Bortniansky's Cherubic Song.

A group of mourners entering the front door as Jocelyn Jones left the funeral home. Together perhaps heading for the suite where the gentleman with the pince-nez was reposing. Walking east to turn down Madison Avenue. The scarfs, shoes, dresses. Past all the old emporiums. Where once one so carefree shopped. The darkness falling on the red and green lights. Feeling so sad, so sad.

The pretzel seller on the street corner. And as I did in college days stop and buy one. At Fifty-Seventh Street cut over to Fifth Avenue. A leisurely stroll down the geographical spine of wealth in this city. All the way back to the great gloom of Grand Central Station where strangers in their endless great numbers pass. Tiffany's and Cartier on the way. Go past a brand new store, a so very English Asprey's, selling anything from platinum toothpicks to gold life-sized eagles. The homeless hiding from the angry black blind man selling pencils because they were invading his pitch. Buy a pretzel from the pushcart man. Chew through the salty crust. College, marriage and family gone. Along with her standards and principles. Even her footsteps sounding solitary. Panhandlers begging everywhere. Be one of them soon. Tears well in my eyes. Rolling down my cheeks. After this. Another strange lonely day, the terrible sadness of which I know I'll never forget.

Because when first she arrived today at the Met she stood on the spacious sunny steps in the warm sunshine. And watching a performing mime on the lower steps. Then her eye caught sight of a terribly young stalwart couple. Of medium and equal height. He blond and she of brown hair. Their soft flowing locks so beautifully groomed against common fashion that they seemed ageless and imperishable against all ravages of life. Reminding of the elegance of her own two estranged children whose silver framed portraits on her bedside dresser still painfully recalled her rejection. And now to see this so young couple, arm in arm, both so handsome and exquisitely in love with one another. She watched them slowly stroll back and forth along the steps. The girl in her tweed suit, he in his tweed jacket and grey flannels. They so appeared to come from another world. For hers had so changed. Then the young couple seemed to disappear. She so wanted to watch them again. But just as she was turning to ascend the two more top steps to enter the Met she felt a gentle touch on the arm and they were suddenly standing on a step lower and directly in front of her. The young man with a gentle smile politely asked if she were Lady Elizabeth Fitzdare whom they were to meet quite near to where she was standing. And she said no but that she wished she were. And the boy with his shining white teeth smiled and said, and so do we wish you were. And it was that that made her weep as she went down Fifth Avenue. Because she might never be again anyone ever again who anyone like that romantic young couple would want to meet.

In getting that day finally to pee in the funeral home she realized that after so much recognition she could never go back there again. But not that far away there was at least a decent hotel to substitute, catering exclusively for females. Christmas was soon coming. She deliberated for days to call the unlisted number of the sad man with the white hair to ask him to drive up the Bronx River Parkway to dinner at her humble apartment and make him a present of a tie. He did say he was shy of the telephone but for her to telephone. And he even said it with a smile, and a please. But with more than half the numerals dialled she lost her nerve again and again. Always at the last moment hanging up the phone. She knew that he did go to a small office and have a secretary. She also somehow knew he had disguised to some degree that he was rich, and she guessed that he might even be extremely rich, added to which was an enormous settlement from the air crash and loss of his family. He occupied a large apartment with seven bedrooms and live-in maid at the East River end of Fifty-Seventh Street and had a view of the tug boats going by. And even putting aside that fact, she knew too that he was a highly ranked Court Tennis playing member of the Racquet and Tennis Club where she'd found herself once up a weekend in New York from Bryn Mawr, having to wait off the lobby in the small ladies waiting room. And it had annoyed her a little as a female to be kept safely out of the club's further inner sanctums. Unless allowed as she was this day to go witness a Real Tennis match which a handful of martini drinking spectators were invited to watch from a little cage at the end of the court.

And now companionship was the least of it. She had to find, really and desperately, another job. And not get fired pouring wine over someone's head. Look every day through the ads in *The New York Times*. Even despondent enough to pretend she was Irish or English and become a housekeeper or maid. Then her children would really have an excuse not to come and see her as they had now not done for more than three months. As someone's domestic servant in one of those vast apartments on Park Avenue around 72nd Street she'd at least have full board, decent coffee to drink and her own bed, bathroom and sitting room. And the way servants were demanding these days she'd insist upon her own private telephone, sound system, television and car to drive. The only trouble was two Bryn Mawr friends lived around there, one with 16 rooms the other with twenty-six. But then gosh, she'd be paid more than a secretary. Plus she'd charge fees for instruction in decorum and courtliness. Or how to shoot her Smith and Wesson from the hip if those two exhibited graces didn't work.

But O god, maybe she'd be met walking the dog in her domestic's uniform by one of the friends on her way to lunch at the Colony Club down the street where her own membership had dismally ceased upon her unpaid indebtedness. O hi Jocelyn I didn't know you lived a-round here. But no. They wouldn't speak. They'd pretend instead not to see me. That's what they'd do. But O god how could she stand it to end up in close proximity and under the thumb of money grabbing gruesomely ill-mannered people flashing around with their jewels and bad taste. What she needed to find was a rich, cultured and not too doddering old man who lived in a big old house with a big old lawn around it and with whom she could listen to madrigals and to whom she could read Swinburne by the fire at night as they sipped their Irish coffee after dinner.

But in scanning *The New York Times* there were no jobs and certainly no old men looking for cultured companions. However there was temporary work advertised in *The Herald Statesman* as an assistant, gift wrapping people's Christmas presents at another novelty store in Yonkers. But by the time she got to and from work on the bus it would almost be preferable to be a whore. Both her children invited by their father to ski at Aspen and then to spend a snow bound two weeks in a cabin out in the wilds of Idaho in the Bitterroot National Forest.

Her sleeping pills were collected. While she brushed her teeth she saw them stacked up ready in the medicine chest of her cramped bathroom. But even though she had not to say please feed my cat, each suicide note she wrote sounded so trite and sentimental. If they were going to be her last words they deserved to be at least somewhat more than matter of fact. Or even unexpurgated. Don't pay that god damn newspaper boy who missed two papers last week any more than the eleven dollars I owe him. Nor the son of a bitch plumber the forty bucks he's claiming to flush a toilet and who thinks he's god's gift to women. And kiss my ass goodbye you bunch of no good low down bunch of shits.

If she could just struggle on till it was February and go see the Paul Klee retrospective. If only she could last that long. And it would also provide an excuse to ask the sad man come with her to the private showing. But she was finding it so easy to cry these days and did right in front of the nice lady who was so friendly at the membership desk at the Museum of Modern Art. Who so kindly escorted her to the ladies rest room and brought her a cup of coffee.

All she needed now was a deep snow-fall with the drifts marooning her in alone with her loneliness. She'd have to phone the boy gardener to come dig her out. O god. A beer now in the Town Tavern wouldn't be the worst thing in the world. Even Clifford, and giving the boy a treat, would be a welcome distraction, if only he'd worked up enough nerve to dodge bullets again. And she really could use a fuck paid or unpaid. Holding a broom or vacuuming or on her knees scrubbing her terribly ugly brown and orange kitchen floor. Get her rocks off for one last time before all her hormones went to sleep.

The mail each day got more and more depressing. Amid the brochures and circulars and bill demands, the Bryn Mawr alumni magazine. Births, deaths and marriages. If the telephone, electricity were added up and paid with this month's rent she'd be broke. But still all her overheads were infinitesimal compared to those at Winnapoopoo Road when she was languishing there. She would never go on her knees to Steve for money. Besides, from what she'd recently read in a gossip column, his new laugh-a-second show was getting drowned out by groans and his bimbo, to whom he was engaged, took off on someone else's private jet to Nice.

However, bills got more and more devastating as they got closer and closer to not being paid and the services cut off. But if she ended it all now her own children could be held responsible for her debts. She had to make sure there was enough money to pay at least a month's rent, and the due bills and her funeral expenses before she could take her pills. And now this morning in the middle of her increasing dread, someone was after her. A registered letter. Her hand trembling as she signed for the mailman. And then as she slit the envelope open with a knife and pinned the letter to the table, her shaking hand then spilt coffee from her cup on the first paragraph.

But other than to nearly shave a groove in Clifford's head she couldn't remember anything else that she'd recently done to be summoned to a lawyer's office. O god Clifford could be suing me for grievous bodily harm occasioned by fear descending a staircase. But this letter isn't threatening. But lawyers don't have to be. They already were. And especially could be if this letterhead is any indication. With offices in Brussels, London, Paris, Rome, New York and Washington. They would be glad if she would please come and see them at her convenience as soon as possible.

Glad could mean anything these days in a legal letter. But the words as soon as possible did not bode well. At least it was no problem that she couldn't phone and make an appointment on the day she was going downtown anyway to visit the Chagall exhibition at the Met. Her last dentist appointment she could afford might have to make her delay an appointment until three o'clock. Maybe her former financial adviser Theodore is going to make at least a partial voluntary restitution of some of the money he's bilked me of in his dud deals and the fortune his meal guzzling team spent at the Bristol Hotel in Paris. One dinner bill alone amounted to eight hundred and sixteen dollars and thirteen cents. And is about what exactly I have left in the entire world before I get cleaned out paying a dentist's bill.

It was bitter cold as she walked towards the East River on Forty-Fifth Street. Across this city that is never dark and when it was briefly once, everyone started fucking. Turn in the doors of this massive skyscraper and into a tropical warmth. One's nose senses the strange not quite noxious smell that new unused buildings seemed to have when the dust has disappeared and the first few polishes have been put on the marble floors. In the pink tiled atrium, shrubbery and flowers. A fountain gushing water into a large pool in the middle of the lobby. A group of these elevators express all the way to the sixtieth, sixty-first and sixty-second floor.

A shiver across her shoulders at the sight of a refined looking lady seated on a stainless steel bench reading *The New York Times*. Obviously homeless with her three polythene bags cluttered about her. But still in proud possession of her dignity. At least enough to keep at bay for a while someone saying get the hell out of here. And I'm going up to the top floor. A sign in New York, that the higher up you go the more affluence and influence to be found. And this firm of lawyers could be nothing but prosperous. Although she'd never heard of them, they had five of those old established New York prestigious sounding names engraved on their vellum over which one tripped one's finger nail. Like her grandmother's lawyers with their two hundred partners and a library bigger than Bryn Mawr's.

Express elevator to the fiftieth floor. Two women and five men, my fellow passengers upwards. And if the girls are anything to go by, although their taste doesn't impress me, they sure make me look not much better than dowdy. The guys sporting all kinds of subtle attempts to be different and not look like lawyers but making sure everyone like them knew they matriculated at Andover, Choate or Deerfield, the latter where her own son had been on the school's winning ice hockey team.

Her ear drums felt the pressure of the altitude and her heart was thumping heavily and rapidly in her chest. The elevator emptying on the sixtieth and sixty-first floors. She had the feeling that arising further alone to the last stop that she was attending upon the holy of holies. And out of fashion now for two years, her clothes so inadequate. And young I once was when once the world was out there and into it you were supposed to daintily step, yellow gardenias in your hair, crinoline aswirl about your feet and as you fox trotted across the ballroom it was only to amuse while waiting until all your dreams came true.

But what had finally come true was that even her very oldest friends were testing her to see if she were still worth knowing. For behind the response to each friendly telephone call she made she knew their thoughts were I don't need to know you anymore. And if I do go on knowing you, you're going to bring me your problems which I don't need because I have my own. And is this, as I alight from this now empty elevator and through this glass door into this spacious waiting room, going to be more bad news of the unknown. Or of the unquantifiable as my grandmother used to say. And as my old bones all sink together in a heap in some old sack, I gather together what optimism is left in my increasingly apologetic self to brave the sternness of this stern receptionist behind her desk. To make sure no poor and homeless soul loiters up here in the clouds.

"I'm here to see Mr Sutton please. I have an appointment for three o'clock and I think I'm a few minutes early."

"Ah yes, it is Mrs Jocelyn Jones."

"Yes."

"Mrs Jocelyn Guenevere Marchantiere Jones?"

"Yes, as a matter of fact."

"Mr Sutton is expecting you. Please take a seat. He won't be a moment."

Sit in soft leather opulence. Open a magazine. Photographs of the glad-faced upon their lawns posed in front of their grand houses and in the splendour of their drawing rooms. And my god, did I hear actually said and well-pronounced, my entire name, just like they announce in court when they sentence you to death. And now I hear the human sound of a hinge closing the bars behind me. But it's a tall wavy grey haired man coming out of a door. And crossing the rug in a dark blue pin striped suit. His hand outstretched and smiling as he slightly bows, and all of her old bones growing fragile in a sack, she stands, they shake hands and he reaches to guide her by the elbow.

"So nice to meet you Mrs Jones. Thank you for coming. I'm Mr Sutton. Do please come this way. I see you're looking at our rug."

"Yes. It's most very attractive."

"It's tapestry Brussels. And those, too, I see you've noticed."

"Yes."

"Paul Klee. An original. And not that we are pretending to the macabre, a Charles Addams. And that's an Edward Gorey. It's nice to have an occasional pleasant distraction to view on our walls."

"Surely more than a pleasant distraction."

"*Touché*, Mrs Jones. *Touché*. Yes I entirely agree. Do please come in. Do. Sit there."

"Thank you."

"Enjoy our view of The United Nations Headquarters and across the East River to Queens and of course if we view from the other side, west to New Jersey and beyond to the Rocky Mountains."

"It's quite stunning."

"Thank you. On clear days of course one can see across Brooklyn and practically follow the aircraft all the way to landing at Kennedy. Being the first tenants and the landlord as a client, we did rather think it nice to be able to get these very top floors of the building. Well I suppose Mrs Jones you're not entirely wondering why, and perhaps to use too strong a word, you've been summoned here. And you are, of course, Mrs Jocelyn Guenevere Marchantiere Jones."

"Yes."

"You mustn't look so apprehensive."

"Well I'm actually in a little bit of a hurry. This is the last day of the Chagall exhibition at The Metropolitan Museum of Art. I've got to cross back over to Madison Avenue and the buses can be so slow uptown this time of day."

"And, Mrs Jones, also going downtown and crosstown."

"Yes. But I do feel a certain disquiet not to say apprehensive curiosity as to what you want to see me about."

"Yes, of course. Please don't let all these files alarm you. It's because of the curious nature of the matter and also that we have had to be somewhat circumspect in alerting you. But some of the mystery is solved. You're clearly an art lover. Just as was Mr MacDurbrinisky. You see we couldn't find any trace of your name in his papers. And I'm sure you won't mind my keeping you if I promise not to keep you longer than is necessary. But if you'd rather we can make another appointment so that you can be with your legal counsel. However, now if you like, you'll be given a full copy of all relevant documents, and I'll just acquaint you with the more salient matters. I'm sure you'll want to listen to what I have to say and so why don't we get straight down to the practical side of matters and I'll move forward as quickly as possible. May I get you some refreshment."

"No, thank you. But what have I done."

"Mrs Jones I know this might all come as a shock to you, especially the very wide extent of assets. But really there's no cause for alarm. We act as Mr MacDurbrinisky's sole executors. Now as you may know with Mr MacDurbrinisky being a very uncommunicative not to say secretive gentleman, few people were aware of his extended business activities which involved a great deal more than the garment industry and his principal product of lingerie and sleepware manufacture."

"Mr Sutton. I really do think I had better tell you that I don't know what you're talking about or what it has to do with me."

"Ah but we're quickly coming to that. But as you may or may not be aware Mr MacDurbrinisky was also the founding finance and seed money in several of America's now well known companies in ventures especially involving such as electronics, British banking and the computer industry. Which explains why a comparatively small garment manufacturing enterprise, much smaller than say the Mitchell Brothers could seem to have made Mr MacDurbrinisky such a wealthy man. In Mr MacDurbrinisky as you know suffering a long kidney illness he sold out nearly the entirety of his interests before his death. And as it would happily appear, very much at the top of the market. So it may come to you entirely as a revelation that as near as can be presently determined Mr MacDurbrinisky's assets may, when finally ascertained, total much more than the twenty-eight million dollars or thereabouts presently accounted for. And as one might aver, we're still counting. Yes. I can see you're very surprised. So are we."

"I would really appreciate, Mr Sutton, you're telling me please what this is all about. Flattered as I would to be a candidate, I hope this isn't some kind of front for the white slave trade. And that I should be ready to run for the elevator."

"Ha, ha, well now I can believe why you and Mr MacDurbrinisky got to be friends and so you must know more than a little of his dealings."

"Mr MacDurbrinisky and I are not friends. And I know nothing at all about his dealings."

"I see. Ah. Well. Not to worry. He was of course very confidential. And I suppose could be regarded, if you'll forgive me for saying so, in view of his considerable wealth, as a rather curmudgeonly and ultra conservative man. As you know there were those who might be tempted to use words stronger about Mr MacDurbrinisky such as penny pinching, however one does not want to speak ill of the dead. But of course as you know he was much disliked by many and indeed as you also know there was bitter and protracted litigation among the family some years ago, happily all settled, although the usual threats and claims have been voiced but are entirely frivolous, which I suppose will explain to you Mr MacDurbrinisky's novel way of bequeathing his money which would

appear and I hope gratifyingly, Mrs Jones, to have result-
ed considerably to your advantage. In fact similar to a
case that I believe happened not that long ago. And may
be happening more than we realize secretly all over America."

"I'm afraid, Mr Sutton, if I may interrupt again. I don't
know of the case whatever it is or was, that you allude to.
I'm listening avidly for a hint of what this is all about but
I still haven't in fact the faintest idea yet of what on earth
this Mr MacDurbrinisky has to do with me."

"O but you were an acquaintance of Mr MacDurbrinisky's."

"I'm sorry unless I'm living out some strange reincar-
nation. I've never heard of, nor come across the man in
my life."

"I see."

"And truly I have no idea why I'm here or what this is all
about. I don't have any outstanding bill for lingerie that I
know of. In fact I've been sitting here in front of your
desk, wondering what I did wrong and why I'm going to
be sued. And how much it's going to cost to fight or set-
tle. Which if it's anything at all I haven't got it."

"I see. Well pardon my chuckle, you're far from being
sued. Or incurring cost, save for our own fees as executors to be paid out of the estate."

"Mr Sutton, I'm sure somehow this is mistaken identity

and it is someone else to whom what you're saying should be said. And if you'll excuse me I really should you know be going."

"Please, Mrs Jones, forgive me if I suggest you should please remain. Of course you're entirely quite free to go but I would advise not. We're anxious to wind these matters up and I think you'll see why when you fully hear what I've got to say. But I can see an explanation is in order. And you will I'm sure see why it was assumed that you knew Mr MacDurbrinisky."

"Well I don't. And no one resembling such a name."

"Well Mr Durbrinisky who was of Russian Jewish extraction and assumed the Mac in front of the name Durbrinisky because of wanting to feel more a part of the St Patrick's Day parade which he always watched from his Fifth Avenue apartment windows. That's a little joke of course. I'm sure he had other reasons. I'm sorry, Mrs Jones, I can see you're not amused."

"No. In fact I'm not. Not because it's not quite funny but because frankly I'm scared stiff as to what is really going on here."

"I do apologise. You see, although nothing could be found pointing to any relationship we were quite certain of your having some personal connection with Mr Mac-Durbrinisky. And I am sorry for our assumption and for the apprehensiveness which I can see this is clearly causing for you."

"Yes. It is."

"Well, brass tacks then and in the customarily alluded to nut shell. Minus disbursements concerning his funeral and some other debts and expenses which are relatively minor, you are, excepting his housekeeper Mrs Kelly, the sole beneficiary of Mr MacDurbrinisky's will, inheriting all and everything of which he was possessed at the time of his death which includes all of the real, material, and intellectual property we have so far traced. You see we in fact would have been in touch sooner following Mr Mac-Durbrinisky's death but we had to deal with one or two nuisance claims and also a matter of another name in the condolence book which has proved on investigation to be fictitious."

"O my god I don't believe this."

"Well if I may Mrs Jones continue. Simply to bring to your attention matters upon which you may like to be immediately aware and matters upon which some prior notice is appropriate. The legacy includes an apartment of eleven rooms and furnishings on Fifth Avenue. Indeed not far down from the Metropolitan Museum of Art as it happens. But perhaps nearer the Frick which clearly, if I may suggest, you may find most pleasantly convenient. And just by the by, the big drawing room, the library which is of some considerable distinction but does involve some delicacy, which we won't burden you with at this time, and Mr MacDurbrinisky's office at home, and the main bedroom suite, all overlook the park from the Fifth Floor and house his art collection. In addition to the main eleven rooms are the servants quarters of three bedrooms and two bathrooms which are self contained. Mrs Kelly, Mr MacDurbrinisky's long time Irish housekeeper presently in residence, is acting as caretaker. She is the immediate beneficiary of one hundred and seventy-five thousand dollars. Her continued employment is at your discretion but she will be entitled to a further payment of one hundred and seventy-five thousand dollars upon her employment being terminated for any reason or the same amount to apply to her retirement. There is also his Rolls Royce which is kept parked in the basement garage of the building directly across the street. Again it's entirely up to you as to whether or not you keep on Steve, Mr MacDurbrinisky's part time chauffeur who also works in the garage. There is a small fishing lodge in upper New York State, Putnam County, consisting of three hundred and ninety acres mostly wooded which includes a private lake of seventy-eight acres where Mr MacDurbrinisky fished. You will have available to you as well eleven crypts in Mr MacDurbrinisky's mausoleum at Woodlawn Cemetery in which he occupies one vault of the twelve therein. It also happens to be among the most elaborately built of recent mausoleums in the cemetery and is regarded as having some architectural distinction."

"If this is someone's extremely bizarre idea of a joke it is entirely a very sick one. And if it isn't a joke then you've got the wrong person. I do actually feel this has gone entirely too far."

"Mrs Jones, please. Do please sit down. I assure you this isn't a joke. I'm a senior partner of this firm. My time is entirely valuable and in fact is priced at precisely three hundred and seventy five dollars per hour. And I further assure you it is not usually apportioned to apply to the frivolous inconsequential. However, I'm entirely ready to confer further in the matter with your own legal advisers."

"But this sounds totally ridiculous. As if I'm going to be arrested or something for impersonation."

"Not if in fact you are the Jocelyn Guenevere March-antiere Jones formerly of 17 Winnapoopoo Road, and removed to apt 6B, 94 Riverview Apartments, Riverview Road, Scarsdale, and now residing at 47 Oneidadeen Avenue, Yonkers. Which latter address is precisely the same as the address as written in the condolence book when Mr MacDurbrinisky's body was lying in wait at the Memorial Funeral Home before proceeding for interment at Woodlawn Cemetery in the Bronx. And I earnestly now assure you that this is not in any way a joke."

"O my god. This is for real. Is it."

"Yes, Mrs Jones, it is. Absolutely for real. And as I anticipated it might, I do understand that it has come as a shock to you."

"Well as much as I still don't believe it, it is I must say

better than being told I'm going to be sued."

"Do I take it then, Mrs Jones, you're ready to hear more."

"Well I guess so. And may I have some water please."

"But of course. Let me pour. There. Now then. I'll continue. Although you will appreciate here that I am skipping over the more mundane. However one must bring to your attention and the reason why time is of some essence, that you have also come into possession of a fairly substantial fully tenanted apartment building on East Fifty-First, the air rights above which have recently been subject to quite substantial and competing offers. Indeed in an amount nearly as significant as the estate itself."

"You really mean this is all going to become mine."

"It is already yours, Mrs Jones. You see Mr MacDurbrinisky's assets were designated in his will to be distributed equally among all those whose names were entered in the condolence book. And, Mrs Jones, your name aside from the fictitious one, is the one and only one so entered. You'll appreciate that the contents of the will were known to myself and one other senior partner of this firm, and neither of us for obvious reasons visited the Memorial Funeral Home. And I suppose it should perhaps form some sort of further explanation to tell you now that I find it entirely understandable that you were not an intimate of Mr MacDurbrinisky's. Mr MacDurbrinisky, although completely honourable, was in fact a very disliked man, for want of use of a stronger and perhaps more disagreeable word. He did too have an eye for the ladies. And certainly, if I may say so, for those as elegantly attractive as your good self. And yes, I must admit I did feel there might have been a personal connection upon that basis. However as it happened you were the only single person other than that person using a false name and address that could not be traced to have paid their final respects to Mr MacDurbrinisky, or indeed, what has transpired according to the terms of Mr Mac-Durbrinisky's will to be the most important of all, to have written your name and address in the condolence book. And I apologise now if this has had, because of its unusual nature, to cause you distress or to have taken up so much of your time."

"I'm still, I'm afraid, far from quite believing all this."

"And that is entirely understandable Mrs Jones. And I apologize to have kept you this long. But I suppose in a way of demonstrating the truth of the matter and getting you to the Met before it closes, just let me see if I can get Mr MacDurbrinisky's chauffeur, Steve. Excuse me. Miss Jinks, see if you can get Steve who works in the garage where Mr MacDurbrinisky's car is kept, and see if he is available to take Mrs Jones to the Metropolitan Museum of Art. Now Mrs Jones it shouldn't take Steve long to get your car here which I can see no good reason why you should not put to immediate and good use. It might not be that faster up Madison Avenue but it will certainly be a lot more comfortable. Ah. Steve. Please. Yes. Mr Sutton. Steve we have Mrs Jones here who has come into the possession of Mr MacDurbrinisky's car and wants to go to the Metropolitan Art Gallery Eighty-First on Fifth as soon as possible. In say twenty minutes. Fine at my office. That's perfect."

"Mr Sutton, I do apologise. I feel now that I've put you to some unnecessary efforts in this matter."

"It's all in a day's work I assure you. And not to sound mercenary I may also assure you Mrs Jones that we shall be adequately compensated in our fees. Indeed ha, ha, you may find yourself saying ouch when you see them. However Mrs Jones if you are late today at the Met I'm sure the curator, a most kindly man who happens to be a friend and to whom you might suggest a modest endowment, might even provide you with a private view after closing hours. But your car should be here shortly. What's wrong Mrs Jones. Are you alright."

"I'm sorry. I'm just I guess finding all this a little bit emotionally wrenching."

"I quite understand. And I hope it's not too inappropriate to suggest at this time that we should be most glad to offer our services in any capacity to you. But of course realizing you may wish to avail of your own legal advisers. O dear, you are alright Mrs Jones."

"No."

"O dear. I can see this has all come as too much of a shock. Would you like to use our rest room."

"Please. If I may. And please cancel the car. I'm just going to go home. And on the train."

"But of course. I quite understand Mrs Jones."

Shown by the receptionist to the ladies room Mrs Jones took a pee in this quite commodious spotless chamber. And Mr Sutton as he passed by the desks of his secretaries, taking notes handed him, showed her to the elevator giving her an encouraging gentle pat on the back as the *ascenseur* door silently slid open, and he smilingly bowed goodbye as they closed. She had his direct dial number and he said for her to be in touch, be she in Paris, Rome or New York, for any help or advice at any time.

She descended sixty-two floors and went through the lobby. The dignified lady with the polythene bags was gone. Someone must have come and said get the hell out of here. She wondered if Mr Sutton knew she carried with her, her thirty-eight, which made a clonking sound when for a moment she put her handbag down on his desk. But she wondered more how this could still be her moving back out on the street ready to go along this pavement, owning a whole apartment house smack in the middle of this city, with people living alive in it.

The traffic thick heading uptown. The foot pavement crowded. A grey gleaming Rolls Royce by the curb, a black coated and capped swarthy man watching the faces emerge as she stepped out of the building and briefly met his enquiring eyes. The name Steve on her lips but would not make a sound. Ironic life comes back to haunt. Her husband's name the same as the chauffeur's. Someone she could now tell to turn right or left, instruct to slow down, command to stop or go faster or even to say to, you're fired. It would be the ladylike thing to do, to phone Mr Sutton to say that Steve might have already arrived and to thank him for bringing the car but tell him not to wait.

Walking west through the friendless anonymous shadows of Forty-Fifth Street to Grand Central Terminal, she bought a pretzel from the pushcart man on the corner. Keep it to chew on the train. Her feet and legs cold and feeling an overwhelming dirge and doom. She could hear again the strains of Bortniansky's choral music and see that face and pince-nez again upon the body in its coffin. On the way to the elevator Mr Sutton said she was now the proud owner of one of the largest collections of pornography in the city. The thought should have made her smile. It instead made her feel more desperately lonely than she had ever felt before.

Clutching three quarters in change in her hand and passing under the vast roof of Grand Central with its painted stars on the ceiling, she recalled the brave volu

ble figures who had come forth in this city to protest at the plan to demolish this massive monument. To save this sacred cathedral of worship to trains and travel. In this city which did have greatness in its buildings and where hardly anyone had ever tried to save anything before. Where the foundations of the skyscrapers go deep down into the stone on this island bourse, where the so many rich can lurk secret in their doormen guarded bastions. Amen.

All was still haunting her as she descended to platform fourteen to catch the four forty-five White Plains train to Scarsdale. Terrified with the barren emptiness of her thoughts. But feeling no despair or misery. Just the invasion of her privacy of another's death invading hers. Which could be now. At last. I can take my sleeping pills. Next month's rent and all bills paid. Make my will. Leave every penny to provide refuge for the dignified homeless indigent of New York. For them to sleep in comfort and rest in peace.

She sat on the left side of the train. A full moon arise this evening heading home on the Metro North and the once Yonkers Division of The New York Central. A social dimension. Ten per cent of people's time in their lives spent going and coming on these trains. The black people coming down from Scarsdale get off at Mount Vernon or 125th Street. The stories of guys every day meeting their girlfriends or mistresses on the train. Years ago it was said you could choose to ride forward or backwards by pulling the wicker seats with the brass handle to face you forwards or backwards. And she'd even found herself greeted by a conductor who got to know her and who said one morning you can call me Dick ma'am, but my full name is Dick Borst. And she could never say good morning Dick. But good morning Mr Borst.

The stations north going by. Fordham, the Botanical Garden and Williams Bridge. Through the dull discoloured window of the train she could just make out the white shadowy shapes of graves and mausoleums along the hillside of Woodlawn Cemetery. Could she bear to be cemented in behind a slab in a sepulchre already containing her benefactor Mr MacDurbrinisky. Yes. Why not. He looked quite gentlemanly in his silk shirt, tie pin and cravat. She'd read someone's reminiscences of the Bronx. About a little boy who said he was paid 25 cents to walk flowers into the graves when people with their bouquets would come up on the Central and it was too far for them to trudge into the cemetery. Whatever was going on in the world then was strange. She heard too there was a lady ghost in flowing robes who was to be seen on misty winter nights along the uninhabited length of Webster Avenue waiting by the cemetery wall and under its big black fence. And cars had stopped to pick her up. To find suddenly she'd vanished from sight.

And what was going on in the world now was the click clack roaring of the train on this crisply cold night. There could be snow. And no doubt about one more day added to her age. Even as a young girl of twenty-two she was already taking steps to try to stop her looking older. And now she was older and ignored and betrayed. When love is gone you can never get it back. And if any of this dream is true one could not now bear to find one again had friends.

Who was she now. A lady of leisure. Who did not have to please, deceive or cajole. Who could afford not to have to be a whore or a nun. And getting off the train tonight the man in the military greatcoat tipped his bowler hat to her. Offered her a lift home in his car. He seemed a little drunk. And getting off the train as she waited for a taxi she saw the girl again who'd been handcuffed in the window of the house in Winnapoopoo Road. She was flanked by two minders. She looked haggard and terrified. And they pulled her into the back of a big black limousine which sped away.

If she rang the sad man who lost his family in the plane crash maybe he would say, why hello, I was just about to ring you. Could that ever be true. That someone would say I was just about to ring you. In order to say would you like to go somewhere nice. What would be absolutely true is that she'd keep the taxi waiting while buying an extra container of milk, salami, salad, cheese and a bottle of beer at the delicatessen store. It could cost three or four dollars or even more than five dollars. And the taxi more dollars.

But tonight no matter what it cost she would buy two bottles of beer. Lonely drink them both by candlelight. Then early to bed. And it's all amazing. Albeit on a lighter note. How when one is able to indulge the luxury of beginning one's life again.

All one thinks
To do
Is end it